ISBN 978-0-259-18318-1
PIBN 10225961

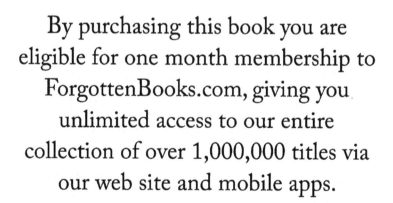

The Trials of the Bantocks

BY

G. S. STREET

JOHN LANE: THE BODLEY HEAD
LONDON AND NEW YORK
1900

UNIVERSITY PRESS · JOHN WILSON

PREFACE

In struggling manhood, as in complacent youth, I have always been fascinated by the Bantock family. We are apt to generalise too freely from meagre experience, and therefore I hesitate to say that all youth is chiefly attracted by exterior things. I had better admit, simply, that my own was so, and the fact that everything in the Bantock household was admirably correct appealed strongly to my youthful sympathies. I say this in humility, not pretending that the excellent qualities of mind and heart possessed by all the Bantocks in their different ways, qualities which I am come in maturer years to understand and venerate, were apparent to my boyish vision. Their town house was in an envied part of London; their country house was the largest and most dignified of its part of a large and dignified county; their dinners were sumptuous but always in good taste; their butler was wonderfully episcopal. Their ancestry, to be sure, did not excite one's imagination, but they went everywhere at the right time and in the most comfortable fashion, and sometimes took me with them. Mr. and Mrs. Bantock alike had a large and unwavering dignity; Maud Bantock's dress — she was seventeen at the time of which I am thinking — was always in the latest fashion and sometimes dazzling; Russell Bantock, my contemporary, was a notable personage at school and in all the best clubs of "the House" in my unpretentious days at Oxford; even Tom, my junior by some years, was always careful to do the right thing in the right way.

It was, as I have said, such exterior things as these — to the exclusion of what is nobler and better still — which fascinated my youth, to my shame or not, as your memory may determine. And even now, when (as I think) the true goodness and beauty of the Bantock life are apparent to me, I am not uninfluenced by the former considerations. In the hardship and anxiety which beset the life of one who writes for bread, it is refreshing and comfortable to turn aside to such a house as the Bantocks'. There one feels that after all there is something solid and permanent in life. As I look down their flowered dinner-table and note the gently-smiling, untroubled faces, and glance aside to the noiseless footmen and imperturbable butler, I feel that, though my own attic crust may haply vanish, so long as the Bantocks live they will dine well. When, trudging on weary feet along Piccadilly, I see Mrs. Bantock leaning back in her soft, swift carriage, and she smiles, faintly but perceptibly, upon me, I feel quite rested. I do not think that if I were reduced to extreme indigence the Bantocks—why should they?—would offer to support me, but somehow my acquaintance with them gives me a vague sense of security against fortune. Merely for this, if there were ever a serious crusade against the rich, I would fight to the death that the Bantocks might continue to have all their little comforts about them. I regret the old days of the patron, and that Mr. Bantock is not mine. He would not read my books, perhaps, any more than he does now, but to feel that my connection with him was something stable and official would be an enduring joy. As things are, if I failed to command a tolerably good-looking suit of clothes, and a shirt that would stand exposure, the Bantocks, though most kind, would, quite excusably—ah, horrible thought! So, you see, the exterior life of the Bantocks fascinates me still, though I know now how little that is in comparison with their inward worth. And yet, sometimes — is it envy of their worldly blessings or a less vile despair of emulating the noble qualities that lie behind them? — sometimes — sometimes it is not altogether disagreeable to reflect that the Bantocks, they too, have their trials in life.

I have made a little collection of these trials, as I have heard of them at different times, and I propose to set them forth with a double object. I wish that people like myself — poor, shifting, unsubstantial people — may observe that even beings so solid and permanent as the Bantocks are tried by fortune: it will be a great consolation. I wish also that they, the aforesaid poor and unconsidered, may see and perpend with what fortitude the Bantocks bear their trials, with what ease they dismiss them: it will be a great

e qualities of the Bantocks,
Skill may fail me, but never

Contents

THE TRIALS OF THE BANTOCKS

I

MR. BANTOCK'S THORN

MR. CHARLES AUGUSTUS BANTOCK is the senior partner in a flourishing and old-established bank, and is in other ways a person whom we all have a natural tendency to admire and love. His father was not a very rich man, and he started life with barely eight hundred a year (he has often told me), and the interest of his maternal uncle, the head of the bank already mentioned. This uncle died when Mr. Bantock was forty years old, and left him a fortune of twelve thousand a year: he was already a partner in the bank. He has been often heard to express his gratitude to Providence that he did not inherit this money when he was a young man, because it might have been his ruin, and poor young men who hear him are greatly encouraged by this to make money, in the hope that they, too, may inherit more. He speaks kindly to such young men. "It's an uphill fight, I know," he sometimes says. "I know it; I've been through the mill. When I started life I had barely eight hundred a year." I do not think it has ever occurred to him that it is possible to have less than that, and one shrinks from hurting his kindly feelings by telling him so.

Mr. Bantock is very different from the man of business whom we find as typical in the books of the last generation. He is well educated, having taken a pass degree at Oxford, and a keen sportsman, generally going to see the Oxford and Cambridge cricket match at Lord's, and playing golf nearly every week when it is fine. He is understood to have a hobby of a serious nature. I think (but am not sure) that it has something to do with science. He never speaks of it, no doubt from modesty. He is of medium height, broad-shouldered and somewhat stout, clean-shaven and benevolent of aspect; he dresses carefully, and has a magnificent fur coat; he is a good husband and father, though he is rightly careful not to give his younger children too much pocket-money, lest they might be tempted to be extravagant and run into debt; he is passionately loyal to his sovereign.

Mr. Bantock's habits are extremely attractive. He breakfasts always at nine, and is in the City by eleven; he seldom leaves it before four o'clock, and allows himself one hour only for lunch at his City club. In the afternoon he plays whist at his club in Pall Mall, for small points, not to encourage gambling, and at seven walks to his house in Grosvenor

Place for exercise. After dinner, in spite of the brain-pressure of the day, he generally reads the evening paper, while somebody plays the piano, or even occasionally goes to the theatre with his wife and daughters, thus doubling their enjoyment of the entertainment. On Sundays he invariably goes to church in the morning, being of opinion that even in town it is a good example, and in the afternoon he sits in his library, which is furnished with all the standard works, and a collection of the *Nineteenth Century*, to which so many well-known people contribute, bound in dark green with red labels. I cannot tell you what he reads, but when Lord Tennyson died, I heard him say that there were no real poets left. On Sunday, too, if there is no dinner-party, he goes to bed early in the evening. On Saturday afternoons, when the weather is fine, he goes to Wimbledon to play golf.

Yet even in this beautiful and useful

life there are trials; and, in particular, I remember a thorn in Mr. Bantock's side, a man called Merryweather. Merryweather was Mr. Bantock's contemporary, and had been his form-mate at Harrow. He used to tell, I believe, some ridiculous story of his having saved Mr. Bantock's life while bathing—I say ridiculous, because it is difficult to imagine that even at that early age Mr. Bantock was so imprudent as to risk the safety of his person. However this may have been, it was no justification for a man in Merryweather's position—he had failed in life, and was the secretary of an obscure and precarious club of a sporting character—when he met Mr. Bantock in the street, calling out, "Hullo, Bantock!" I question if there was another man in London, not of an assured position in society, who would have called Mr. Bantock "Bantock." But Merryweather had no subtle perceptions. He looked rakish, with his hat on one side, and seemed entirely to lack that reserve which is so rightly valued a feature of the English character. He laughed quite loudly in the street; if he argued with a cabman it was not in the tone of quiet authority which you and I use, but in the high-pitched voice of one who loves a contest. He was altogether unsuited to be Mr. Bantock's acquaintance. But ten years ago, Mr. Bantock, in a moment of thoughtless generosity, asked him to dinner. I met him on that occasion; I was young at the time, but even then my sympathetic instinct divined the horror of the Bantock family. Merryweather was excited; he laughed uproariously; he told foolish stories about people I am sure Mrs. Bantock would not care to meet. Nothing could stop him. Mrs. Bantock looked at him; Mr. Bantock looked at him; Russell Bantock looked at him; I looked at him; Merryweather went on.

Of course he was not asked again; and, indeed, never again passed the threshold of Grosvenor Place. Both Mrs. Bantock and Russell Bantock spoke seriously to Mr. Bantock of the unwisdom of knowing him; and Mr. Bantock, who, in spite of his position, was a genuinely humble-minded man, was guided in such matters by his family. He tried to avoid Merryweather, but—through timidity, his wife hinted, but I know his kindness of heart was the cause—could not bring himself absolutely to cut his unfortunate acquaintance; indeed, he would have found it extremely difficult to do so.

He was cruelly requited for his kindness; for Merryweather was continually meeting him in Pall Mall and elsewhere, greeting him with a noisy laugh, and sometimes even slapping him on the back. I have seen the victim of such a shoulder-slapping ruffian turn round and strike his assailant; but Mr. Bantock was too gentle for this. He would nod, courteously but with finality, and pass on. But Merryweather would not allow this; he would walk by his side telling him atrocious stories, and as it were, involving Mr. Bantock in his unseemly joviality. Sometimes Mr. Bantock would take refuge in a cab, thus missing the exercise so necessary to his health. I have known him arrive in Grosvenor Place quite unnerved. There was one terrible scene, when Mr. and Mrs. Bantock, with Lord and Lady Addleshaw, were dining at the Savoy, previously to going to the play. Merryweather passed their table, on his way to a party of quite odd-looking people (Mrs. Bantock told me), and greeting Mr. Bantock loudly, as usual, slapped him so violently on the back that the glass of sherry he was in the act of drinking was upset into his soup. It must have been a dreadful moment; Mrs. Bantock cannot refer to it without emotion. I am glad I was not there. On another occasion, while Mr. and Mrs. Bantock were walking in the Park, Merryweather's large dog, recognising in Mr. Bantock a person with whom his master often spoke, raced up to them, and (it was a very muddy day, I regret to add) put his paws on Mr. Bantock's white waistcoat. There were other instances almost as distressing, but I cannot bring myself to relate them. Enough to say that for several years Merryweather continued to be a thorn in Mr. Bantock's blameless flesh.

But like all trials patiently endured, this one came to an end. Merryweather sank even lower, lost his appointment, and had a serious illness. Then the true nobility of a forgiving spirit shone forth in the Bantocks. Mrs. Bantock gave me a commission to buy a pound of grapes, and to leave them at Merryweather's door with her card. And when Merryweather was well again, Mr. Bantock got him a small post in a bank, connected with Mr. Bantock's own, in the Colonies, and he has troubled my friends no more. But Mr. Bantock's dignity under the infliction of Merryweather was one of the grandest things I have ever seen.

II

THE DREADFUL GOVERNESS

THERE is no one in the world towards whom I have a more humble feeling of reverence, I had almost said of self-abasement, than I have towards Mrs. Bantock. This is, I hope, chiefly due to my appreciation of her extraordinary excellence. I have known her for twelve years, and, so far as my observation extends, she has never done anything wrong, anything in the slightest degree to be censured. Her history, so far as I know it, is a calm succession of admirable incidents, a history surely to be far more warmly admired than those exciting and tumultuous lives of which we sometimes hear.

Mrs. Bantock was the daughter of a wealthy but not ennobled brewer, and in

r youth she had all the advantages which
dignified home and the most accom-
ished governesses and masters can
ve. I have no doubt that she pos-
sses all the accomplishments, intellect-
l and artistic, which are suitable to a
dy, though of course at her age and in
r position there are few occasions for
eir exercise. I have never known her at
loss for an opinion on any social, polit-
l, or literary question, even in regard to
atters which her many occupations have
evented her investigating, and her opin-
n may be always accepted as final —
· my part, I never dream of disputing

She married Mr. Bantock when she
s twenty-five years old, bringing him a
·tune of five thousand a year, and has
en a devoted wife to him, so that he has
ver had recourse to those anti-domestic
axations, such as gambling and going to
e less respectable places of amusement
which even middle-aged men and men

of position are sometimes known unhappily to indulge. She has been an excellent mother; her sons have gone to the best schools and colleges, and her daughters have had the best and most carefully selected governesses. To her servants and dependants she is a friend; not, indeed, committing the false kindness of overlooking faults, but being always ready to assist them with wise counsel. She is most charitable, being on the list of vice-presidents of many excellent institutions, some of them patronised by royalty itself. But I should weary you, though not myself, if I recounted all her virtues. In a word, she is a well-nigh perfect woman.

In my first acquaintance with her I experienced a feeling of timidity which has never quite worn off. It may have been (I hope it was) partly due to the unconscious recognition that she was a being superior to myself. But it was without doubt largely due to the majesty of her appearance. Mrs. Bantock was tall, somewhat stout, and extremely dignified in her carriage. In the years since I first met her she has become stouter, and that has added to her dignity. She was, I have heard, a beautiful girl; in her middle-age she is handsome, and her features express the—so well employed—habit of authority. Certainly I was once afraid of her in spite of her kindness; I hesitated to venture a remark in her presence, and was confused when she addressed me. To this day, when she holds out her hand to me I feel presumptuous in shaking it; I feel that it would be more seemly were I to kneel and touch it with my forehead or something of that kind. I admit that she patronises me; I would not have it otherwise; it would seem altogether wrong that Mrs. Bantock should address me as an equal. There are many people by whom a plain man must expect to be patronised in modern England, such as novices in aristocratic society, Stock Exchange Jews, and the lesser lights of the stage, and I confess that such people sometimes irritate me. But when Mrs. Bantock patronises me I am merely grateful.

In fact, my only complaint in this matter (not that I do complain) is that Mrs. Bantock is too kind in noticing me. She will sometimes catch my eye at a small dinner-party at her house and drag me out of a preferred obscurity to ask, "Are you working hard?" My reply is inaudible, and she adds, "When you publish another book you must send it to me." (She is very kind in this particular, not only accepting my books, but even asking me for additional copies to give away.) I murmur how glad I shall be to do so, but by this time she is talking to somebody else, and I sink relieved into obscurity again. Such notice embarrasses me. But her kindness is usually most tactful, and, especially, it often takes the form of allowing me to be of service to her in a humble way; she knows, no doubt, what gratification such service is to me. Thus I sometimes receive a post-card in the morning telling me to get her tickets at some theatre. Now this is really kind, because, of course, a footman could get them quite as effectually as I; but Mrs. Bantock knows that I have tried to write for the stage and am therefore interested in it, and knows also that I am at a loss how to employ my time in the morning. She has promised, by the way, that if ever a play of mine is pro-

THE DREADFUL GOVERNESS

I was staying with the Bantocks in the country, when there arrived a new governess for Ethel, a girl of thirteen. This was Miss Clavering. She was a young woman of twenty or so; her appearance was entirely unobjectionable, and, I am told, her references were all that could be desired. I would not malign her, in spite of the pain she gave us all, and I therefore admit that she seemed to be accomplished, and was well-bred and amusing in her conversation—as a rule. She had high spirits—an excellent thing in its proper place—and Ethel, I am told, was devoted to her. But on the very day of her arrival she amazed and scandalised us. She argued with Mrs. Bantock at lunch.

It happened that the conversation turned on Thackeray—Tom Bantock was reading *The Newcomes* as a holiday task—and Mrs. Bantock observed that he was too cynical. Whereupon Miss Clavering leant forward in quite an excited way and said: "Oh, do you think so? It always seemed to me he was too sentimental." Mrs. Bantock has a wonderfully equable temper; she merely said, with dignity: "It has always been understood that he was a cynic." That surely ought to have closed the discussion, but Miss Clavering went on: "But don't you think that what has been always understood is often wrong?"—a pretty sentiment for a governess! As in the case of Merryweather, we all looked at Miss Clavering, and it was equally useless. Mrs. Bantock, of course, ignored her question. But the unfortunate young woman began to give instances of Thackeray's sentimentalism, and appealed for confirmation to me, thus placing me in a very awkward position. Mrs. Bantock at once turned to me. "You agree that Thackeray was a cynic?" she said. Then, of course, I could hesitate no longer, and agreed cordially. That ended the discussion, though Miss Clavering looked quite contemptuously at me,—a most unwarrantable proceeding.

It is my experience of life that when Thackeray and his cynicism have been mentioned, Dickens and his vulgarity are never far off, and, sure enough, at afternoon tea they made their appearance. Once more Mrs. Bantock and Miss Clavering were in collision, the latter taking up the position that to describe vulgar people is not in itself vulgar. This time I voluntarily went to Mrs. Bantock's assistance. My argument, I admit, was sophistical, but I think the circumstances justified it, and Mrs. Bantock rewarded me with a smile. When Miss Clavering had left the room Mrs. Bantock expressed an inclination to tell her that it would be more comfortable for her to dine in the schoolroom, but Mr. Bantock, to my surprise, interposed, and we expected dinner with sinking hearts.

It was quite terrible. The conversation turned on the stage, and Mrs. Bantock said how glad she was that Ibsen was over. In her opinion, she added, he ought never to have been allowed. Immediately Miss Clavering began to argue. This time, however, she hedged — which was cowardly, I thought. "Of course," she said, "I don't admire everything he has written, but it seems to me impossible to deny that he's a great dramatist." Mr. Bantock, who treated Miss Clavering throughout with great good-humour, contented himself with remarking that she would think differently when she was older; but Mrs. Bantock, I could see, was extremely annoyed. It so happened that in talking apart to Miss Clavering before dinner I had agreed with her on this very point, and the dreadful girl at once drew me under fire. My respect for the Bantocks — almost my sense of duty — impelled me to deny what I had before affirmed, but somehow I had not the nerve to do so, and I echoed Miss Clavering's opinion, though I am thankful to say she must have found me a very feeble ally. Mrs. Bantock stared at me, and I literally trembled, spilling some salt. Mr. Bantock said he had thought that I was too sensible for that sort of nonsense; he showed me none of the tolerance he had shown the ringleader in the disturbance. When we said good-night, Mrs. Bantock did not smile.

I tossed on my pillow all night, and felt wretched and very nervous the next day at lunch, when for the first time I met Mrs. Bantock and our persecutor again. But Mrs. Bantock made me ashamed of my trepidation, so noble was the calm fortitude she displayed. She addressed a remark or two to me, for which I was inexpressibly thankful. She was, however, most rightly cold towards Miss Clavering, merely replying, "Indeed," when spoken to by that irrepressible young woman, who for her part showed no contrition whatever, but chatted gaily the whole time, chiefly to Mr. Bantock. But lunch passed without an argument, and we looked forward to the rest of the day with cheerful hearts. We little knew what was to happen that very afternoon.

It is impossible for a sane imagination to conceive of Mrs. Bantock in any ridiculous position whatever, but more especially in one physically ridiculous. Even a position in which people differently constituted would not be ridiculous, but which, owing to her stateliness and imposing presence, would make Mrs. Bantock appear less dignified than usual, is quite unimaginable of her by a normal mind. Some of the most terrible nightmares I have ever had have been those in which (my nerves, doubtless, being morbid from overwork) I have dreamed of Mrs. Bantock scrambling up a precipice, or even (horrible to relate!) swimming in the sea, though of course properly attired. Awake, and in my right mind, I cannot see such distressing visions — except when I remember that terrible afternoon. Miss Clavering was giving Ethel a lesson in lawn-tennis, when Mr. and Mrs. Bantock walked slowly past the court behind Ethel and in front of Miss Clavering. Russell Bantock and I were sitting on a bank near. Anybody but Miss Clavering would have stopped; she called out in a cheerful voice: "Please don't come so near, I'm teaching her to take them off. the end crease, and I'm afraid of hitting you!" The next minute it had happened. A ball, hit by Miss Clavering, came full at Mrs. Bantock; she saw it coming, and, to avoid it, had to duck her head and run for several steps. I started to my feet, but on reflection thought silent sympathy the better course and sat down again. Miss Clavering ran

Irs. Bantock apologising, as well
t. Mrs. Bantock walked silently
ouse. You will hardly believe me
ell you that after a minute or two
avering went calmly on with her

Mrs. Bantock later in the after-
d she confessed that her nerves
n much shaken, but assured me,
anxious enquiries, that she felt
d. And the heroic woman ap-
t dinner as though nothing had
d. One would have thought that
ength Miss Clavering would be
. Not at all! She argued again,
: disagreeing with Mrs. Bantock's
of the growing want of respect
o their natural superiors by the
'ders. Miss Clavering said they
not be expected to admit that
ly who happened to be rich was
tural superior. I was more on
rd that evening, and came to

Mrs. Bantock's assistance with such success that I am glad to say she smiled quite kindly at me. But the strain was telling on us all.

However, it was not to last long. The next day Mrs. Bantock declared that her digestion was upset by Miss Clavering's unaccountable proceedings; and Mr. Bantock, knowing the terrible consequences of such a calamity (which even impaired Mrs. Bantock's usually perfect temper), agreed that Miss Clavering must go, and on the fourth day from her arrival she went.

I have tried to forgive her, and think I have succeeded, even to the extent of forgiving the cruel remark I heard she had made since of me,—that I was "a cowardly parasite." But Mrs. Bantock's forgiveness seemed to come without an effort. A very few days afterwards she began to joke in her inimitably witty manner about Miss Clavering. "My dear," she said to a friend, her neighbour, Mrs. Lupin, "she contradicted everything I said, and nearly killed me with a lawn-tennis ball." And when, about a year later, we heard that Miss Clavering was engaged to be married to a young baronet whose sister she had been teaching, Mrs. Bantock wrote her a charming letter of congratulation, and I believe will be quite willing to go to her wedding. Such is the charity possible to a perfect woman!

III

THE ORDEAL OF RUSSELL BANTOCK

I KNOW no more respectable young man, no one more absolutely correct in every relation of life, than Russell Bantock, Mr. and Mrs. Bantock's eldest son. Even at school this distinction of perfect propriety belonged to him. He was not in the cricket or the football eleven, nor was he even in the sixth, but he attained to the average in both spheres necessary to the respect of masters and boys, and was never in anything approaching a row. His friends were among the most eminent boys of our time; but eminence in school life was not by itself a passport to his intimacy. If a boy was a hero in the field, or a distinguished member of the sixth, Russell Bantock was always affable to him and counted him among his friends, but he was never really intimate with him unless he were assured that the boy's social position "at home," as we said, was quite what was to be wished. He sometimes made mistakes — as who of us does not? — but he always did his best to remedy them. I well remember the tact and firmness with which he gradually cooled towards a boy whom he had believed to be the son of a Member of the existing Cabinet, but whose father he subsequently discovered was a mere literary hack who did not even belong to a good club. The boy's casual mention of Brixton as his home and a subsequent consultation of a Court guide, found on our house-master's study-table, had opened Russell's eyes to the true state of the case.

It may be supposed from what I have said that I wish to imply too great an importance for myself, since Russell Bantock invited me to stay with him in the holidays. That is not the case; I am sure it was only a fortunate accident that procured me the honour which was to bring with it so many agreeable consequences. It happened at the time I was invited that Russell was preparing for his matriculation at Oxford, and as I was two forms higher up in the school and accounted a fair scholar, I was able to be of use in reading with him. I refer (in modesty) my frequent intercourse with the Bantocks to the same cause, in the case of Russell's subsequent examinations at Oxford and those of his younger brother. Mrs. Bantock has assured me that she considers me quite a valuable friend of the family, and I am more than repaid by this gracious acknowledgment for any little exertions I may have undergone. I may also mention (again in modesty and not to boast) that she has been so kind as to employ me as a sort of informal secretary in the clerical work (for which, of course, she has no time) consequent on her position in the charitable world.

But to return to a more important subject than my own accidental merit. At Oxford, Russell Bantock's correctness was even more admirable than at school, and was attended with even greater success. From the very first he was extremely exclusive. This was perhaps rather a bold step to take, but like most bold steps, firmly and consistently made, it succeeded. He rapidly became a member of the very best clubs in his college, "the House," and in the University at large. The more general life of the place, which would have brought him into contact with unselected people, he did not affect. For example, "the Union" was not in our time a fashionable resort; I believe that to the end of his time at Oxford, Russell pro-

fessed that he did not know where it wa:
He did not care much for games, but h
was known to hunt occasionally, and s
escaped the odium which men who "did n
do anything" incurred; he succeeded, lik
his father before him, in taking a pass de
gree. He was never known to boast c
his money; on the contrary, he was i
the habit, like his father, of confessing in
limits. "I'm really not a rich man," h
used to say; "my governor only allow
me seven hundred a year." His lunche
were excellent, but he always (and es
pecially after his first year, and when h
position was thoroughly well establishec
was careful to avoid lavishness.

When he left Oxford, Russell wa
called to the Bar, not intending to prac
tise, but because he thought it was due t
him to be a member of a learned profes
sion. He then went into the Bank, an
was made a junior partner almost at onc
I know no young man about town wh

leads a more careful life. He rides every day before breakfast; he plays billiards or pool in preference to cards because the former games involve a certain amount of exercise; he dances sometimes in the season (though only at very good houses), but otherwise never stays up late or commits any kind of excess, except on Saturday nights, Sunday being a day of rest. His private income is at present only two thousand a year, and in his opinion that is an insufficient sum on which, in his position, to marry; in a few years it will be considerably increased, and then, I believe, he will add his influence to the institution of matrimony; in fact, I know that he has already fixed on his future house, though not yet on the lady. In this matter he is wisely careful not to commit himself, being aware that in the course of a few years his inclinations might change — unless, indeed, a peculiarly desirable person (in point of rank or money) were to be attainable, in which case he has told me in confidence that he might hurry matters to an earlier issue. I need hardly say that he belongs to two irreproachable clubs. He has little time for literary cultivation, but keeps up an acquaintance with contemporary letters by reading the reviews of new books in *The Times*, and he has told me that he would be quite charmed to meet a few of the better-known writers of the period, simply as writers, and not counting those whose social position would make them in any case people one likes to know. In fact, Russell is an accomplished and admirable example of English young manhood: he is business-like and far-seeing, and, not disdaining the amusements natural to his years, he pursues them with unvarying discretion. His principles are simply beyond criticism.

Up to a few years ago, however, I had never seen Russell Bantock put to stern proof in the war with circumstance. It happened at last, and since then I have estimated his occasional friendship at its right value. It was on a Sunday morning in June. I was due to lunch with the Bantocks that day, and as I walked up St. James's Street I saw Russell on the steps of his club. I saw at once that something had happened. He explained in a few words; it was, indeed, a thing to try the strongest patience. In that year (I must premise) many men wore short black jackets with tall hats, but, of course, it was possible to wear bowler hats with these jackets as an alternative. Well, it seemed that some culpably careless member of Russell's club had gone in there with a bowler hat (pot hats they are also called), and on going out had taken Russell's tall hat, leaving his pot hat behind him. Now, Russell was wearing a frock-coat. You see the tragedy at once. No one knew whither the evil-doer was gone;

in fact, no one was certain who it was. Russell could not deliberately take another member's tall hat. But it was impossible that he could wear a pot hat with a frock-coat. To wear one at all on Sunday morning in the height of the season in Piccadilly outraged every fibre of his nature; to wear it with a frock-coat was, as I have said, impossible. But what was to be done? Russell thought of staying at his club until another tall hat should arrive from Grosvenor Place. I suggested, however, that we might take a cab, and he might go in it without a hat; people could suppose that he had uncovered on account of the heat. After some misgivings he consented to do this; we went down the steps of the club and nodded to a cab.

At that moment (the stars in their courses fighting against my much-tried friend) Lord X. came up. Now, Russell was slightly acquainted with him, and no ıbt would have been glad at any other e to cement the friendship. Lord X. very rich peer (the fourteenth earl of family, I believe), a great racing man, y popular, and among other things on committee of a club for which at that e Russell was standing. But Lord X. ılso very unconventional, not to say :ntric, concerning things which seem him to be unimportant. I have no bt that if it were convenient to him walk down Piccadilly in knickerbock- no consideration of propriety would vent him.

Oh, Bantock," he said, "you 're the man I wanted to meet." Russell, I ld see, was pleased by this address; little do we foresee our troubles, even most prudent of us! "I hear," con- ed Lord X., "that your father's king of taking a moor this year. I k I can let him have Strathpellan."

That will be capital," Russell said.

"Yes, but there are certain things to be explained; things he'd better understand before he thinks it over. I can just as well tell you, and you can explain to him."

"Certainly," said Russell; "won't you come in here?"

"Afraid I haven't time," replied Lord X., taking out his watch. "No; I'm due at the Wellington—lunching with a man. There's time to walk, though. Look here; are you going home? Well, let's walk together," including me with a glance, "and I'll explain as we go."

"But," said Russell, "but—I should be delighted—but—I've no hat."

He explained the hat tragedy. Lord X. was certainly very dense; he only said: "Well, but the other chap's hat fits you, I suppose, if yours fitted him. Bring that hat," he called to a waiter, who was on the top of the steps. We knew it fitted; it was by that, the tall hats having been examined in vain, that we knew it was left by the appropriator of Russell's.

The waiter brought it, and Russell put it on with a bitter smile.

"That's all right," said Lord X., with heartless cheerfulness. "Come along."

"But I can't walk down Piccadilly in a frock-coat and a pot hat," said Russell.

Lord X. laughed — positively laughed. "You young men are much too particular," he said; "it will do you good. What on earth does it matter? Come along."

Russell looked at me. I knew how terrible a struggle must be going on behind his mask — so splendidly indifferent. At any other time he would have liked very much to walk down Piccadilly with Lord X. But now! Think of it! It was Sunday morning, at the height of the season, about half-past one. Piccadilly would be full of people coming out of the Park. Think of Russell passing

Hyde Park Corner in a frock-coat and pot hat! I remembered in a flash how, a little while since, he had decided to cut a man he saw in Pall Mall who was wearing a cutaway black coat (merely) with a pot hat, even though it was pointed out to him that the man was fresh from Australia, and might not have known — instinct should have taught him, Russell said. Imagine Russell's feelings now! On the one hand, the risk of annoying Lord X., and possibly (his peculiar ideas considered) of incurring his contempt; on the other hand, the certainty of an outrageous appearance and the dread of misconstruction by his friends. The presence of X. did in a way save the situation, but everybody who knew Russell might not know X. by sight, and it would be impos-

Russell was for keeping on the Green Park side of Piccadilly, but X. said: "Let's cross; I like to see my friends." So in obedience to this fatuous good-humour we walked along by the clubs and the houses, meeting a throng of people coming from the Park. It seemed as though the whole of Russell's acquaintance was there to mock him. He had continually to smile, as best he might, and take off his abominable hat. Meanwhile, Lord X. pursued his vain chatter about Strathpellan. I have always admired the Spartan boy who said nothing of the fox that gnawed his vitals, but what was he to Russell Bantock? I watched him; his face was calm; every now and then he made an intelligible reply to Lord X. But, of course, when he had an opportunity, he stopped for a

moment to explain his distressing c
to his friends. And even that sligl
gation was presently denied him.
the third occasion Lord X., with
inconceivable brutality, exclaimec
you mention that hat again I shall
it in; I'm sick of it." Russell
lip, but took the brutal hint.
word of reproach did he say, and
only twenty-six years old! At l
reached the Wellington—it see
week to me, to Russell it mus
seemed a year. Lord X.'s last
was: "You'd better put that ha
glass case and tell the story to your
children." It might have been a
recognition of heroism, but I fear
but silly sarcasm. We hurried
Grosvenor Place and the ordeal wa

IV

BAD COUSIN CHARLOTTE

THE Bantocks are singularly untroubled by poor relations. I suppose they have some; in fact, I know of a few. But I have never met them in Grosvenor Place. Perhaps they are conscious of an inferior refinement which would be too evident there; perhaps they have committed the indiscretion of asking the Bantocks for money. That offence, I know, would not be forgiven. Mr. Bantock takes an interest in the housing of the poor, and in the various schemes, from time to time suggested, by which the working classes might secure (by their own thrift) a pro-

charitable institutions. But both are vividly conscious of the evils of individual assistance to the needy, and aware that such acts of seeming kindness are really selfish and a wrong to the community at large. I remember an occasion on which an application for such assistance was discussed. Mr. Bantock was very firm. "I have worked hard for my money," he said — Mrs. Bantock, with conjugal tenderness and admiration, interposed: "And you do still" — "And I don't see," he continued, "why other people should get money without working for it too." And Mrs. Bantock seemed indignant at the idea that the results of Mr. Bantock's toil should be diverted from their proper application. I surmise, then, that their poor relations may have been so wrong-principled as to ask for money — it is an evil habit of poor relations — otherwise I cannot account for my not having met them. For, as I shall presently show, the Bantocks are full of the kindly feelings of kinsmanship.

Cousin Charlotte is a rich relation. She is the daughter of Mrs. Bantock's paternal uncle, who married a member of an old and well-known family. Her parents are now dead; she is about fifty, and unmarried, and has no brother or sister. Through her mother she is related to a number of the people whose family histories are such edifying and agreeable reading in the peerages. The Bantock feeling for kindred and expansiveness of heart embrace all these people more or less. "So-and-so, who 's a sort of cousin of ours, you know," is a phrase one frequently hears in their house. In fact, I happen to know that Mr. Bantock has once or twice remitted in their favour his principle of never lending money. Cousin Charlotte spends June and July in London, and August and September in the country, at one house or another, in

England; during the rest of the year she dashes about the continent of Europe, which I hope (if I may permit myself a mild sarcasm) enjoys her society; I do not like her. And yet I must confess that she has some excellent qualities; she seems to know everybody and to go anywhere; her conversation is often extremely clever; she is very well read, and has a remarkably good taste in pictures and music.

But her faults! I hardly know with which to begin. The fact that the Bantocks cultivate her assiduously is a wonderful proof of their kindliness, and sense of the sacredness of relationship, for she never comes into their house without saying some outrageous thing, and I have seen Mrs. Bantock, usually so calm, flush with annoyance at her speeches. That is perhaps her greatest fault,—her outrageous frankness. I cannot believe that she means all she says; it is enough that she says it. One would almost suppose (only it is too absurd) that she despises the Bantocks, and thinks them prone to selfishness or snobbishness — the latter a vulgarity of which, as Russell Bantock says, nobody is guilty nowadays. She laughs at Mrs. Bantock's charities, and at Mr. Bantock's hard work; she speaks of Russell's invariable correctness as though it were a sort of crime. On one occasion she took an extraordinary liberty with me. We were leaving the house together, and she said: "I often meet you here. I suppose you like a free dinner." I suppressed my annoyance, and replied humorously that I did. "Well," she said, "I should have thought you'd have found it cheaper to dine at your club." I have not the least idea of what she meant, but the interference with my pecuniary affairs I thought most ill-bred; my affection for the Bantocks alone prevented me from saying something sarcastic to her.

But such personal offensiveness by n
means exhausts her conversational lapse
The Bantocks are above all things r
spectable, and naturally therefore pref
to think that people of position, and e
pecially those whom they have expresse
a desire to know, are respectable als
Cousin Charlotte tramples on this exce
lent feeling. Thus when Mrs. Bantoc
expressed a kindly wish to meet Lad
Sunnington: "Like to know Peggy Su
nington, would you?" Cousin Charlot
roughly asked. "I don't think you
better; she'd be a bad example to yo
girls. She's a rake, and a mercenary o
too. All the Fonthill women are.
There was a pause after this painful r
mark, — an injudicious pause, since
gave Cousin Charlotte an opportunity
launching into a lamentable account
the Fonthills' indiscretions, to use
harsher word. Another of her dreadf

money, a thing the Bantocks (except for some useful purpose) are always careful to avoid—it is so vulgar. She gives distressing accounts of the impecuniosity of well-known people, seeming almost to make the Bantocks' well-earned riches a reproach to them. Another irritating habit she has is to talk of her Bohemian friends, of whom, I am sorry to say, she seems to have a considerable number; she does this especially when other people are dining at the same time, and when, of course, the Bantocks would much prefer that she should talk of her relations or her really nice friends. Of course, as Mrs. Bantock once said to me, these Bohemians may be very clever and all that, and some of them are perfectly respectable, and one meets them at the best houses—still, it is much nicer to talk about one's own world, as it were, and really Cousin Charlotte might give people a false impression. And this reminds me of another fault. Mrs. Bantock, in her beautiful spirit of hospitality, has sometimes suggested to Cousin Charlotte that she might bring one of her friends to dinner to make up a number, or for some reason of that sort; well, on these occasions, Cousin Charlotte, instead of bringing one of her really nice friends, almost always brings some Bohemian person whom the Bantocks have no desire whatever to know in private life. On one occasion she brought to lunch a man who gave public entertainments: I left the house a few minutes after them—they walked away together—and I passed them at the corner of Park Lane, and I am certain that Cousin Charlotte was trying to persuade him to make the Bantocks the subject of one of his sketches. It may seem incredible that she could have been so lost to all good feeling, but I am certain of the fact.

To do Cousin Charlotte justice, she

ılly affords proof that she is not
:r insensible to the affection and
ıtion shown to her by the Ban-
She is generous in a material
When Tom, whose career at
hurch was wilder than his brother
; — I mention this with regret,
ıs merely the defect, I am sure, of
cent light-heartedness, so charm-
other ways — when Tom left
considerably in debt, Cousin
: sent him a cheque for a sub-
ıum, and though there was a sus-
bout it of a desire to encourage
ɔe less correct than his brother,
ıts allowed him to accept it, grate-
When Maud Bantock married,
Charlotte gave her some beautiful
Such tokens of a better nature
ıt have weighed with the Ban-
ɔr Cousin Charlotte has never
ɔpped, but on the contrary is
eceived with kindness. In this,

as in other matters, the Bantocks rise superior to those feelings of vexation to which lesser people succumb.

I may, perhaps, give a more adequate idea than as yet I have given of Cousin Charlotte's strange perversity of conversation by repeating what was said at dinner one night, Cousin Charlotte and I being the only guests, and Mr. and Mrs. Bantock, Ethel, Russell, and Tom being present. I have not described Cousin Charlotte: she is tall and rather stout, in fact, not unlike Mrs. Bantock, but with far more animation, or rather with far less dignity and stately repose. She is large-featured, with what is called a Roman nose; she wears pince-nez; her voice is loud and somewhat harsh and excited, so unlike Mrs. Bantock's quiet, authoritative tones; she gesticulates freely with her hands, again unlike Mrs. Bantock, who keeps hers, when not in use for eating and drinking, folded in her lap. Altogether she is a disagreeable contrast, except in figure, to that admirable woman. Cousin Charlotte looked up from her soup and said abruptly to Mrs. Bantock: "How's that Home of yours you made me subscribe to?"

"It's nearly all settled," Mrs. Bantock said; "we debated to-day about the food."

"Oh, what did the debate turn on?"

"Chiefly whether they should have meat once or twice a day."

"And which side were you on?"

"Oh, against their having it twice. Quite unnecessary."

Cousin Charlotte laid down her spoon. "Good heavens!" she exclaimed with a sort of foolish violence. "I can't imagine how you have the—what shall I call it?—the power of abstraction. I daresay you're right economically and all that—but how you can get over the contrast! You go down there after an immense lunch—"

"My dear Charlotte—"

"I don't mean to be rude—a very good lunch, let us say. You go down in a fat carriage"—her epithets are generally irrelevant—"with a grossly over-fed coachman—I've seen him—and you proceed to determine that forty poor old women shall only have meat once a day. I can't understand it."

Mrs. Bantock replied to this nonsense with quiet dignity: "I fail to see what connection my lunch and the coachman's meals have with—"

Cousin Charlotte interrupted her rudely: "Of course you do. And economically the connection is very indirect, no doubt. But the fact that the contrast did n't strike you—"

Mr. Bantock came gallantly to the rescue. "You're a Socialist, Cousin Charlotte," he said. She turned on him angrily. "No, I'm not. You don't see my point. It's simply that anybody can have the calm assurance—that's why I never could go in for that sort of thing. I only mean that Flora"—Flora is Mrs. Bantock's name—"is a better philosopher than I am: that's all."

She smiled, I suppose in tardy apology, and the subject I thought had dropped. But presently Cousin Charlotte recurred to it quite excitedly. She asked suddenly: "What do those poor souls get to drink?"

"Water," replied Mrs. Bantock, "sweetened, if they prefer it, with a little lemon cordial."

"Oh, that's too bad," said Cousin Charlotte, very rudely: "I don't think you ought to have deserted beer!"

There was a dreadful silence: I looked hard at my plate. Then Mrs. Bantock, laughing rather forcedly, but with extraordinary good nature, asked: "How do you mean—desert beer?"

The terrible woman explained—right

out. But I must add in justice to her that the servants were not in the room.

"Why, Flora," she said, "if it was n't for beer, where would you and I be? You owed your food, your clothes, and your roof to it till you were twenty-five, and you owe a quarter of your income now. As for me, I owe the whole of mine to it—beer, bless it!"

Perhaps I ought to apologise for inflicting such terrible vulgarity upon you; it may be too realistic. But imagine the feelings of the Bantocks! I took a swift glance round the table. Mrs. Bantock sat flushed and silent; Mr. Bantock had made an heroic effort to laugh; Ethel looked down at her plate; Russell was frankly disgusted. Only Tom laughed naturally: he called out, "Good old beer!" At any other time I should have thought the exclamation unworthy of him: at that moment we all felt dimly that he had saved the situation. A sort of laugh ran round the table, and I earned (I hope) Mrs. Bantock's gratitude by changing the subject—to my own cost, for Cousin Charlotte immediately began to contradict me.

I rather despised the proneness of her mind to a trivial detail, to which besides she seemed to attribute an absurd sentiment. For at the end of dinner she suddenly went back to the beer question. "Flora," she said, "if you'll let those old women have beer twice a day I'll subscribe another twenty pounds a year."

But Mrs. Bantock had been justly annoyed. "Impossible," she said; "beer is quite unnecessary." The ridiculous Cousin Charlotte positively began to plead. "Do," she went on, "do. It's on my conscience. I shan't go to bed happy unless you agree. I can't enjoy eight thousand a year made out of beer if I don't prove my faith in its virtues. Look here, Flora, if you'll let them have the beer, I 'll give you this ring I picked up in Venice." She drew off her finger and passed to Mrs. Bantock a very beautiful old ring. Mrs. Bantock was naturally tired of the silly subject. "Oh, well," she replied, "if you 're so anxious as all that—" She put on the ring and smiled kindly on Cousin Charlotte, as she rose, in token of reconciliation. As I held the door I admired her completely restored equanimity.

Now this is a very mild instance of Cousin Charlotte's outrageous behaviour. I have heard her say far worse things than her allusion to beer. But it may serve to show to what annoyances the Bantocks are exposed in their love of kindred. With smiling faces they brave such things about once a week for two months every year.

V

THE PREMATURITY OF HENRY SOMERS

It is an example of my friend Russell Bantock's native generosity of mind that as a boy he was never able to understand that a gentleman could be without means. As he grew older he had to realise that it was sometimes the case, but he only came to such a recognition by degrees. He granted, at first, that a man who had a title, or was son or nephew or first cousin to one who had (I am stating the matter roughly, but it came to that), might be a gentleman and yet have no money. Later on, he supposed that a man who was indubitably a gentleman and yet without money either had lost his money or had not yet come into the money he was des-

tined to have. I have seen his face
sometimes when his father has been
ing the circumstance that he begꞔ
with only eight hundred a year, bu
he remembered his father's present
ence (even in these dark days destir
arrive) and his face cleared. But
only within quite a recent date, and
protest, as it were, that he has bee
to admit that a gentleman possibl
not have, have had, or be going to
money. And by "money" he mea
income sufficient, in his own be
phrase, "to do things decently." I
sometimes wondered if he made an
tion of my own case; I think, I
that he did.

Since he has had to recognise th
fact of the conjunction of gentlema
with poverty, he has been very bitte
the neglect of certain people who (a
tlemen, in Russell's generous th
ought to have money, somehow or

to procure it. He is extremely angry with the people who, in pursuit of some alleged ambition of merit in art, write or paint things which do not sell, when they might (conceivably) make money by painting or writing something else. He is inclined to be sceptical about the said ambition, and to think that what prevents their money-getting is mere incapacity, and, indeed, I agree with him that the people who might, but do not, make money in this high-principled country are extremely few. But he is more angry still with the people who marry on insufficient means — on less, let us say, than two thousand a year. To marry on a thousand a year is, in Russell's opinion, gross carelessness; to marry on less than that is an act of criminal folly. In his own case, as I have mentioned, he thinks two thousand a year altogether insufficient.

Imagine, therefore, his decorously expressed, but keenly-felt indignation when, some few years ago, his sister Maud announced her promise to marry a man who had only five hundred a year! Mr. and Mrs. Bantock were equally angry, no doubt, but I think that with Russell the wrong went home more bitterly. He loved his sister. This cruel thing that she contemplated was a crushing blow. Everything that man could do — but I anticipate. I am able to give a complete history of the affair from the beginning, for both Mrs. Bantock and Russell confided in me freely concerning the various moves in the game — if one can call such a disastrous business a game — valuing, I hope, my complete sympathy with their sorrow and appreciation of their wisdom. Maud Bantock's fellow-conspirator in the infamy — it is best to call things by their right names — was a young man called Henry Somers. He had been a contemporary and acquaintance of Russell Bantock at Oxford, and to this fact owed his introduction (so ill-requited!) to the Bantock family. His parents died when he was a boy, and left him an income of five hundred a year. Now this was all very well in his youth; it enabled him to be in a fairly good set at Oxford — more or less, in fact, in Russell's own. But as an income on which to marry Maud Bantock —! Yet he had no more, and his only other asset was an Australian uncle who might leave him money, but would not promise to do so, and declined altogether to give him an allowance. He had been called to the Bar, at the time of his monstrous proposal, and professed to be working hard in the chambers of an eminent barrister; but, of course, he could not expect to get any considerable practice for himself for some years.

On the other hand, Maud Bantock could not expect any considerable sum for dowry. In the first place, the Bantocks lived nearly up to their income, and

Mrs. Bantock often said she did not know in what way she could possibly economise, consistently with their position. In the second place, it was the ambition of both Mr. and Mrs. Bantock, but more especially of Mrs. Bantock, that Russell should take eventually a place in the world worthy of his parentage and talents, and for that nearly all the money they had would be required; in other words, he was to inherit almost everything and to found a family. There was, therefore, little left for Tom, who was destined, at that time, for the Church, and for the two girls. It is true that if either of them were to be sought in marriage by a very rich man who insisted on a substantial dowry, or by a man of really unexceptionable position in society, her parents would have stretched a point, as would have been reasonable. But it was absurd for Maud to think that they would go out of their way to encourage such a deplorable marriage as one with Henry Somers.

However, that audacious suitor went calmly to Mr. Bantock and expressed his wishes. Mr. Bantock told him that his income was altogether insufficient, and advised him to talk it over with Mrs. Bantock. He actually had the insolence to go to her. At first, as she told me, she could hardly believe her ears, and then thought he must be joking, but he assured her of his seriousness. Now, Mrs. Bantock, generally most careful not to hurt people's feelings, can be in a good cause remarkably frank; she told Somers plainly that he was a fortune-hunter. He did not take the rebuke in good part, but forgot himself so far as to be quite rude to Mrs. Bantock, and he made the idiotic assertion that he preferred Maud not to have a penny. Thereupon, Mrs. Bantock for his own sake, as well as that of everybody concerned, forbade him the house. Somers uttered something very like a defiance, and went off. That, as it were, was the first act.

Russell was at once informed of the disaster, and his sister not being present — for one of her very few faults was a somewhat hasty temper — freely expressed his disgust with Henry Somers, who ought, he said, to have known better; but you never, as he said also, know what these middle-class people will do. I am not sure in which sense he used the term middle-class, but I supposed he discarded the ordinary classification (by which he and Somers would have been on a par) in favour of a more subtile and genuine distinction: but I am digressing. Maud Bantock was summoned, and directly, to the consternation of Mrs. Bantock and Russell, sided with Somers, and announced, with tears, her intention of marrying Somers or remaining a spinster. That was terrible: what was to be done?

At first, in his manly rage, Russell proposed to horsewhip Somers, but reflected that Somers would certainly make a vulgar fight of the proceeding, which would have been annoying. He then decided, much against the grain, to interview Somers in a less violent manner, and went for that purpose to the Temple, where Somers lived. Russell described the interview to me afterwards. He began by asking Somers if he were mad, and Somers answered, brusquely and rather rudely, that he was sane. Russell then enquired on what he proposed that Maud and himself should live. He replied on his five hundred a year until he should make money at the Bar. Russell pointed out the impossibility of this plan, and Somers replied that it was not at all impossible; they would live, he said, in a little flat somewhere; they would have enough to eat, and even for rational amusement, in a quiet way.

Russell told me he felt it useless to argue with such imbecility, but he did ask Somers how they could possibly entertain. "Oh," was the foolish answer, "we shall entertain one another and such of our friends as are not dependent on a butler for the entertainment." The folly of this stung Russell to say that Somers was not acting like a gentleman, whereupon Somers, with inconceivable brutality, told him to leave the room.

The next step, since Maud remained obdurate, was that Mrs. Bantock wrote to Somers to say that the best course would be to wait for a year, during which he was not to go to Grosvenor Place nor correspond with Maud, and that then they would see what could be done. Somers was quite insensible to the generosity of this proposal. He replied (without even thanking Mrs. Bantock) that he would be no better off at the end of a year, and saw no reason for waiting. He added, in his dull, prosaic, legal fashion, that Maud was of age and could choose for herself. Mrs. Bantock, Mr. Bantock, and Russell then appealed to Maud's sense of duty, of propriety, of piety, to wait a year. Finally she consented to this, a concession which, to some extent, restored one's injured confidence in her. But I ought to say that I believe her original foolishness was inspired by a quality good in itself, though misplaced. I would not deny her share of the Bantock virtues, though, perhaps, she has shown less regard for me than the others. Mrs. Bantock became cheerful again; she was convinced that time and the wise exclusion would cure the poor girl of her infatuation for one who, Mrs. Bantock impressed upon her, was quite unworthy in every way. And so ended the second act of the comedy, if the word can be used of occurrences so painful.

About this time bad Cousin Charlotte arrived in town, and Mrs. Bantock appealed to her for sympathy. With her usual perversity she at once declared herself on the side of Somers, who, she chose to say, seemed to be a sensible and spirited young man. I heard a fragment of conversation which seemed to turn on the matter as I entered the drawing-room after dinner. Cousin Charlotte was speaking to Maud. "And you consented to wait a year?" she was saying. "Ah, well then, my dear, perhaps it's as well you should wait. If you'd refused I'd have helped you: I won't now till the year's up." Mrs. Bantock looked very angry indeed at this open encouragement of folly. I will not repeat, though I cannot retract, the word I used before. But Cousin Charlotte's stay in town was that year very short, and she did no particular harm. She went and we breathed again. Maud remained docile.

The third act came a month later. It was a joyful and altogether satisfactory act.

But its opening was ominous. I had, one afternoon, the pleasure of meeting Mrs. Bantock at the house of a mutual friend, and she kindly permitted me to walk back with her, to carry some books she had borrowed of her hostess. As we neared the house in Grosvenor Place a man was seen to descend the steps. He came towards us: it was Henry Somers! We stopped instinctively, amazed. Mrs. Bantock looked sternly at him. He came up with a brazen smile, taking off his hat.

"Mr. Somers!" she exclaimed, "I thought it was agreed—have you actually been to my house?"

"Yes," he said, with horrible cheerfulness,—I noticed at this point that he was apparently excited about something.—"I was sorry to miss you. Miss Bantock was out too."

"You asked for *her!*" Mrs. Bantock exclaimed in just indignation. "Mr.

Somers, this is contrary to every idea that a gentleman — "

"Yes, yes," he interrupted, "but I thought you would n't mind for once. The fact is, I came to say good-bye. I can't wait this year; so I came to release Maud and say good-bye for ever, and all that. I 'm going out of England to-morrow." Mrs. Bantock, who has a very kindly nature, became more friendly, and held out her hand. "Good-bye," she said; "you 'd better write to Maud and explain; it is for the best."

"By the way," said Somers, as he shook hands with her, "I hope you 'll be interested to hear my uncle in Australia 's dead and left me his money. It's between seven and eight thousand a year. It's quite true," he added, no doubt noticing Mrs. Bantock's surprise; "here 's the cable." Mrs. Bantock read the telegram and returned it to Somers. She seemed hardly to know what to say.

He put it calmly in his pocket and began to move off. Then Mrs. Bantock, thinking, I suppose, of her child's happiness, spoke. "Stop," she said; "come in and talk to me. You can't mean —"

"I'm afraid I can't," the unconscionable Somers answered: "I've an appointment. I meant what I said." He smiled, took off his hat, and before another word could be said was walking away.

Mrs. Bantock walked on slowly to the house; she was slightly flushed, and did not speak. She stopped at the steps. "Go after him," she said; "say I want to speak to him. If he won't come, ask him to come to dinner, say I particularly wish it. That will show," she said to herself, but still aloud, "if he means it — he can't mean it." I rushed up Grosvenor Place, overtook Somers, and gave my message. He laughed, with a horrid sort of sneer. "Oh, say I shall be delighted to dine," he answered.

It seems that the little speech he had made about saying good-bye was actually his idea of a joke, a sort of "score," he has been heard to say, over my friends. It was almost inconceivably bad taste, but Mrs. Bantock, for the sake of her child, forgave him that, as she forgave him all the pain his premature conduct had cost her. His uncle was really dead, had really left him the money. He married Maud Bantock at the end of the season, and I believe they are happy. Still, I cannot help thinking that a man of his eccentricity and cynicism (as shown in the wretched five-hundred-a-year business) is not a good son-in-law for Mrs. Bantock. However, though he and Russell have never been really reunited, she has never—since the afternoon I have described—uttered one word of complaint.

VI

TOM'S PROFESSION

PERHAPS the gravest trial I have to record of my friends — worse than Merryweather, than Cousin Charlotte, even than Somers in his five-hundred-a-year days — was occasioned by the extraordinary proceedings of Tom Bantock on his leaving Oxford a year ago. There is something, if not in names generally, at least in those by which people call their relations or intimate friends: it may be significant that while Russell Bantock was never called anything but Russell, his younger brother was always known by the heartier but less dignified name of Tom. There was certainly a great difference between the two brothers. As a boy at school, Tom, though sometimes in scrapes, seemed to be quite correct in his general ideas and behaviour, but, in the freer life of Oxford, he quickly showed that he did not share Russell's perfect prudence, and when he came down for good it was found — alas! — that he could not emulate, nay, that he even despised Russell's absolute correctness in every sphere of life, — in deportment, in amusements, and in the choice of acquaintances. I would not blame Tom too severely; he was cheerful, high-spirited, and good-natured, and these lighter virtues may to some extent be set against the more sterling qualities of his brother, whose preoccupation with correctness does, perhaps, result in a demeanour a trifle too severe. But at this period poor Tom went very much too far.

As I have related, it was the intention of Mr. and Mrs. Bantock that Russell should inherit nearly all his father's property, and take an even higher position in English life; he was to go into Parliament later on, and it was hoped, by his wealth and superior talent, would die the first of a line of titled and securely settled Bantocks. So that Tom could not expect more than a moderate allowance. It was intended that he should go into the Church: there was a living attached to Mr. Bantock's estate in the country, and it was hoped that Tom might rise to be a Dean or a Canon, and in that way contribute to the position of his family. When he first went to Oxford, Tom acquiesced in this really nice idea for his future, though without much enthusiasm. But then came that natural and excusable — on the ground of his beautifully joyous temperament — but most unfortunate period of wildness, most unfortunate indeed for the plan entertained for his future, since it resulted in his being sent down for good at the end of his second year. The difficulty was not, of course, insuperable. After a decent interval, and residence at a theological college, Tom might still have been ordained. But a greater difficulty arose: Tom refused to go into the Church. He said that he was not fit for it, and had no inclination for it whatever.

Everybody argued with him. Mr. Bantock pointed out that in the Church he would be comfortably provided for in life; Russell insisted on the necessity that a man who is not rich should have a profession undeniably that of a gentleman; I think Mrs. Bantock enlarged on the good he would be able to do. For my part, I explained to him over and over again that those who are wild in youth often make the best clergymen. He would listen to no argument, and mine he even repelled with a contumely which I am determined to forget. It had finally to be acknowledged that, for Tom Bantock, the Church was no longer in question.

What was to be done? Tom seemed to have no idea on the subject at all. He said that he would not mind reading for the Bar, but Mr. Bantock was convinced that he would never make money at that, and, in any case, it must be a long time before he could. The army was possible by way of the militia, but that was an expensive course, and one likely to encourage Tom in what seemed to be constitutional idleness — I regret to say. Russell objected to his going into the Bank, foreseeing troubles and complications from his presence there; besides, there would be no room for another partner, especially for one who brought in no capital of his own. The Stock Exchange was suggested, but nobody believed in Tom's capacity to make money there. And it was stated forcibly by Russell, in an extremely wise argument, wise beyond his years, that while commercial pursuits were excellent for the younger sons of the aristocracy, for the younger sons of those whose position, however excellent, was in a way based upon money, the profession, as such, of a gentleman was imperative. If only Tom could be made the secretary of a statesman — one with good social connections — or if an opening could be found for him in the diplomatic service! But, alas! no such opening presented itself.

Meanwhile, Tom stayed at home doing nothing, and, I regret to say, vexed the peace of the Bantock family by sordid discussions about money. His habits were extravagant. He did not spend, of course, so much money as his brother, but he spent it so foolishly — so wickedly, as Mrs. Bantock was obliged to tell him. That is to say, he would give dinners to people whom he professed to like, but who could be of no use to him socially, at all, and he would go and bet at race meetings to which nobody went,—nobody, that is to say, except those who were interested in racing. Then, again, he would disappear for a week or two, and it would leak out that he had been hunting,—a pursuit in which, it is true, he met some really nice people, but which was not worth the money he wasted on it. Of course, he soon found himself in pecuniary difficulties.

I remember very well the painful scene which ensued when this fact first became known. As it has been related, Cousin Charlotte, showing for once her better nature, had paid Tom's debts when he left Oxford; since then he had received an allowance which should have been ample for his needs. Well, one morning I went early to Grosvenor Place, Mrs. Bantock having honoured me with a commission to investigate some cases on the list of a charitable society of which she was then the energetic secretary. I called, in obedience to a post-card, to take down the names and addresses. I found Mrs. Bantock, Russell, and Tom in the dining-room, finishing breakfast, and was aware at once that some discussion of an unpleasant nature was in progress. As I entered the room, Russell said: "We'll discuss it some other time," but Tom said, "Oh, *he* does n't matter,"—a remark which showed that after all Tom appreciated my friendship,—and the discussion went on. It seemed that Mr. Bantock had received that morning an intimation from a money-lender that unless a certain sum—over a hundred pounds—borrowed by Tom, was paid at once, an action would be brought against Tom. Mr. Bantock had gone to the City before Tom was up, and had deputed Mrs. Bantock and Russell to speak seriously to him. The discussion went on, and I report it verbally to show what poor Mrs. Bantock and Russell had to endure at this time.

"It is infamous," said Mrs. Bantock, "after all we have gone through on your account!"

"Oh, *you* never went through anything. Cousin Charlotte paid."

"If you insult me," Mrs. Bantock said with dignity, "I must leave the room."

"Well, but look here," the misguided young man exclaimed, "it's a beastly shame. Russell has two thousand a year, and I only have five pounds a week."

"My good fellow," Russell answered, with admirable good-humour, "in the first place I'm your elder brother, and in the second place I do some work."

"Oh, rot about elder brother," returned the incorrigible Tom; "you talk as though the governor were a Duke. And as for work, you don't do as much work in a week as the cook does in a day, and that's more skilled work than yours into the bargain. It's beastly unfair."

Russell, of course, ignored this absurd

tirade, but Mrs. Bantock interposed on his behalf. "Your brother," she said severely to Tom, "spends his money profitably; you waste yours." Tom was ready with a wickedly senseless retort. "I know," he said contemptuously; "he spends his money in making a show and ingratiating himself with people who would n't care twopence about him if he was poor. Russell 's a snob." Russell could afford, of course, to ignore this ridiculous charge which he had often, quite unnecessarily, repudiated. But he was naturally offended, and got up and left the room. Mrs. Bantock continued to speak gravely, but kindly, to Tom.

"You can't expect your father to pay this," she said. "But, of course, something must be done. Perhaps your Cousin Charlotte —" Here Tom rudely interrupted. "Why should she?" he asked, forgetting what kindness Cousin Charlotte owed his family. "I simply can't ask her. The governor must pay; it's ridiculous to make all this fuss. You can spare it easily, if it comes to that, and I could have a decent allowance if he did n't have all those confounded servants and carriages and rot." And then he proceeded, to my consternation, to make a personal attack on his mother, and, with a strange, unconscious irony, strange even in one so unfortunately distraught, he chose the very point on which she proves her superiority to a common, but disastrous failing, that is, not giving way to her native generosity and humouring people's vices and extravagances, especially, as an ordinary mother might, those of a younger and less worthy son. "Why," he said brutally — I must really call it so — "if you gave me a quarter of the money you spend on dress, as any other mother would, I should be all right."

I expected that Mrs. Bantock would crush him with a well-merited rebuke, but I estimated her wonderful patience too low. Instead she made a good-humoured joke, and said, "I should like to whip you!" But Tom answered rudely: "Do; the exercise would do you good." Mrs. Bantock rose and turned to me. "Come to the drawing-room," she said, "and I'll give you that list. I can't stay here to be insulted." But Tom interposed. "All right," he said, "I'll go." He left the room, slamming the door. I thought, when he was gone, that even Mrs. Bantock might break down, after all this brutality shown to her by one she loved. But I was mistaken. She turned at once to other matters and began with a remark which showed her kindness to myself, an heroic courtesy which added, if anything could, to my admiration for her. "I'm afraid," she said, "that Shoreditch *is* rather a long way off. It's so good of you to go for me: I could n't find time myself. I'm really quite grateful to you." And, if she showed some acerbity, a little later on, over my slowness in grasping all the details of the charitable cases, as she dictated the matters into which I was to enquire, that, I am sure, was due to my own stupidity, not to any loss of temper in herself.

I learned afterwards that Mr. Bantock paid the money-lender, but intimated to Tom that he must find work on penalty of losing his allowance. And then came poor, mad Tom's crowning act of disregard for the feelings of his family.

I was dining, a few weeks later, with the Bantocks, who were alone. Dinner was over, and everybody was content, when Tom, who had been, I thought, smiling to himself in an ominous manner throughout dinner, exploded a horrible bomb. "You'll all be glad to hear," he said, with almost diabolical calmness, "that I've found some work. It's got to do with the only thing I really understand, — horses. A man I know, Robinson, who's a livery-stable keeper, has given me a post as shower-off of horses. That means I shall drive those kind of skeleton waggonettes you see with carriage horses in them, and I shall try the paces of horses he buys, and that sort of thing. It's a very good thing for me."

No one spoke. Tom leaned back in his chair and sipped his port. Mrs. Bantock broke the terrible silence. "Do you know what you're saying?" she asked. "Oh, yes," said Tom, "I never get drunk here." Russell tried to open his eyes with sarcasm. "Of course," he said, "you think that a thing a gentleman can do." It was quite thrown away. "Oh, yes," said Tom, "it's honest work, or if there's any cheating about it, that's the boss's business. It won't disgrace my long line of ancestry." Then Mr. Bantock found words to clothe his indignation. "Do you mean to tell me," he asked, "that you propose to be one of those people driving those things I see about the street? Do you think I should recognise you?"

"Don't trouble yourself," answered Tom; "in fact, I'd rather you did n't distract my attention from my horses." "Tom!" said Mrs. Bantock, almost tearfully, "you'll break my heart with your cruelty. Have you no regard for my feelings?" "Have you no regard for your mother?" shouted Mr. Bantock: I had never heard him shout before, and admired his beautiful loyalty to his wife. "Well," said Tom, "I did my best: I waited till after dinner. But I don't see why anybody should complain. You all bully me to get work: now I've got it. I defy you to prove it's not as honourable as being a clerk in an office." Mrs. Bantock said: "You know we can never allow it." "Well," replied Tom, flippantly, "make me your coachman instead. I should do quite as well as that fool you 've got." Mrs. Bantock rose. "Once for all, Tom," she said, "if I hear another word of this, you leave the house."

We had a most uncomfortable ten minutes when she was gone. I tried to make a diversion, but nobody took any notice of it. Russell said presently: "In my opinion, Tom, it would be best if you were to emigrate." And Tom burst out, "You selfish brute! If you say that again, I 'll kick you." He rose and Russell looked alarmed, not, of course, for himself, but for fear lest he might have to chastise Tom. But Tom simply left the room. I had never felt so uncomfortable at the Bantocks' before, and I confess I felt ill-disposed towards the author of the distress, poor, mad fellow that he was. He gave up his foolish idea the next day, but with a bad grace, on threat of the failure of all supplies. But his vocation in life still remains a problem. Every effort is being made to have him appointed attaché somewhere, but so far without success. Even this great trial, however, is borne by the Bantocks with outward calm. If we all could imitate them!

VII

MOSS

I HOPE that, in my account of the Bantock family, I have not given the impression that they value mere wealth, as such. That would be a cruel slander. Of course, for the beautiful life they lead — a life of which it is my ambition in some sort to convey the atmosphere to you — wealth is necessary. But they would be the first of all people to disclaim the vulgarity which cares for mere money when it is not united with refinement. I have heard them speak with disdain of people, far richer than themselves, who lack refinement; people who are not really nice at all, and know nobody. Even for worldly success, as Russell once pointed out to me, "It's not enough for a man to be rich, he must have tact as well." Consequently, as I have said, they contemn even the very rich when their riches procure them nothing but vulgar pleasures.

A striking application of this admirable principle was afforded by the case of a man called Moss. Moss was of very humble origin and of no literary education. He had left England, I believe, in the capacity of assistant to the cook on board the steamer in which he sailed. He had made a large fortune in Australia: in the beginning, I have heard, by opening a small eating-house in the vicinity of some newly-discovered mines; then by importing thither champagne, of his own manufacture, in enormous quantities; and, finally, by the acquisition of mines and the formation of numerous companies. At the time of this relation, he was newly returned to his native country; as illiterate and, I should think, even more vulgar than when he left it, but immensely rich and in a position to confer favours on people by giving them early information about his companies. For example (I explain for fear you may be ignorant of these matters), if Moss were to inform you that, by applying at once, you might acquire shares in a new company, and you did so, you were quite certain to make a large profit by selling them when he informed you that their price was at its highest; a brief period after which they would decline in value very considerably. I say that Moss was in a position to confer these favours. I am bound to add that he very seldom conferred them, preferring to make all the money himself, and that he not infrequently failed to give the selling-out order until the shares had gone down with a rush. Well, Russell met this Moss man in the City, and formed a sort of acquaintance with him; he invited him to dine at his club — at the inferior of his two clubs — and at Grosvenor Place, and shortly afterwards, when the Bantocks were on the point of leaving town for their country house (it was at the end of the season), he suggested that Moss should be asked down for a few days.

Immediately the true refinement of the Bantocks appeared. Mrs. Bantock said emphatically that Moss was a vulgar little man and quite impossible. Mr. Bantock and Russell at once agreed with her. And this, in spite of the fact that Moss had at least four millions of money!

But, of course, it is one thing to be conscious of a man's vulgarity, and quite another to refuse to invite him to your house. Russell adduced many arguments why Mrs. Bantock should not refuse. He believed that Moss might be induced to grant the Bantocks some facilities in the way of investments and some profitable business in connection with the Bank;

and therefore, he said, they should be grateful to the fellow — even in advance. It would be a kindly action to invite Moss to the country at once, because, being so lately arrived in England, he knew almost nobody outside the City, whereas he was not likely (such is the sordid condition of English society) to remain in that condition for long. It was therefore essential, if they wished to be really kind to him, to ask him at once, before he was taken up by other people. The invitation would certainly please him; he had never been in a country house, at least since his early youth, when he held a subordinate post in the stables of one, and even then he never penetrated beyond the kitchen. This little sally on Russell's part amused us all very much, but his serious arguments convinced his parents of the wisdom — the kindness, rather — of his suggestion. Mrs. Bantock consented to ask Mr.

Moss to the country. "There's one mercy," she said; "the man hasn't a wife." But she went on to lament the divorce of wealth from refinement. "There ought to be a law," she said, "against people like that having money at all!" Russell, however, was more tolerant, and remarked that Moss was not such a very bad fellow, after all. "We can't all be gentlemen," he added generously; "Moss is quite a good-natured little man." Indeed, when it had been decided to invite him, it was generally agreed that Moss had redeeming qualities, and it seemed almost as though the Bantocks wished to excuse their kindness towards him; but that, surely, called for no justification.

I am bound to say that Cousin Charlotte seized on this little point (when she heard of the invitation) and distorted the Bantocks' motives with a perversity I thought almost disgusting, and which, I am sure, she cannot have meant seriously. "Oh, what's the use," she said brutally, "of pretending you like him? You know you think him an objectionable little beast, and you only ask him to get what you can out of him." "How can you say such things, Charlotte?" Mrs. Bantock interposed, justly offended. "Oh, I don't blame you," Cousin Charlotte went on; "everybody does it. It's very clever of you to be first in the field and choose your time. In a few weeks, he won't think anything of you; he'll know a lot of people with fat titles, and won't look at you then. Why, even I could be of more use to him than you. Don't be alarmed; I won't try to cut you out. Yes; it's very clever of you. But you ought to make sure of the *quids pro quo*"—she condescended to this vulgar joke!—"Have you got an agreement in black and white?" (Of course nobody answered this coarse question.) "You should have. He 's sure to do you out of it, if he can. It 's all a matter of business; everybody does this sort of thing nowadays — more 's the pity. I don't blame you, my dear Flora; only don't, for Heaven's sake, talk cant about liking the little brute." I think Cousin Charlotte's comments were almost the worst part of the trial caused by Moss, but he himself was a dreadful infliction.

I travelled down with him from Charing Cross. Our cabs drew up at the same moment. He was a little, fat, oily man with beady eyes and a monstrous nose; about forty years old. He seemed to have been lunching well, and was jovial in manner. "Come along," he said; "my man 'll get the tickets. You don't mind travelling first class?" I wondered if he would present me with my ticket, but when I tendered the money to him, he accepted it without demur. His conversation on the journey was not agreeable. "Let's see," was one of his remarks, "you write things, don't you? What do you call it — author, aren't you?" I did not notice in him, by the way, — as, indeed, I have never noticed in anybody, — that awe of literary people with which the illiterate are sometimes credited in books. I replied that I was an author, in a sort of way. "Isn't much in it, is there?" he asked. I did not quite understand what he meant, but I answered that it was a matter of opinion. "I mean, you don't get much out of it, do you?" he continued. "For example, how much a year do you suppose you make?" The sum was so trifling that it seemed almost indecent to mention it to a millionaire. However, I told him. "My stars!" he said; "why, a bar-man in Gamboolie makes more than that. Why on earth don't you chuck it?" I replied feebly that I liked it, and he gave me a look of undisguised contempt. During the rest of the journey our conversation was fitful and limited.

But Moss's spirits, depressed by his temporary association with one so poor as myself, revived when he saw Russell at the station. They greeted each other with great cordiality. Soon, however, Russell needed all his self-control to support Moss's garrulity and frankness, and there was a moment when I thought it would give way. We passed a pretty country girl, and Moss leaned out of the carriage to inspect her at greater advantage. "That's a nice piece," he said, — by the way, I make no attempt to reproduce the peculiar offensiveness of his accent and mispronunciation, — "one of your village belles, eh?" "I'm sure I don't know," Russell answered shortly. "Get out! *You* know all right; you're a judge," the dreadful man rejoined, and gave a loathsome wink. Russell bit his lip, but restrained himself admirably. I confess that when we reached the house Moss was more subdued. I think he really had some feeling of proper awe for Mrs. Bantock. Even during dinner he was tolerably silent and respectful in his manner towards her and Mr. Bantock, and I really began to like him better.

His demoralisation began with the arrival of Cousin Charlotte, the next day. My feeling that something painful would happen did not deceive me. I heard her talking to Mrs. Bantock before dinner, Moss not having appeared. "The man 's bored to death," said Cousin Charlotte. "You must contrive to amuse him somehow, or he won't do anything. I saw him yawn to himself five times at tea-time." "I 'm really so relieved," Mrs. Bantock said; "he 's so much quieter than I expected — much more subdued than he was in London." "My dear creature," returned Cousin Charlotte, — fancy calling Mrs. Bantock a creature! —

"I tell you he's simply bored. I don't suppose he's a bit impressed by your grand manner and all that, and when he gets among people who play practical jokes with him, he'll hate the idea of you. If he were enjoying himself, he'd make a noise. I shall draw him out."

Dinner that night was terrible. The Bantocks had carefully abstained from referring to Moss's past, especially the early part of it; Mrs. Bantock had said she supposed that Australia was very interesting, but that had been the only reference to the topic; the conversation had been about nice and interesting people in England whom Moss ought to know, but since he did not know them at the time, his share had been small. Cousin Charlotte changed that excellent state of things altogether. She at once began to question Moss about his early days in Gamboolie, and the social habits of the miners. By rapid degrees, Moss became garrulous and even confidential. Cousin Charlotte put him quite at his ease by laughing and asking questions in an interested manner, and, under her encouragement, Moss grew louder and louder, and more and more detailed. It was most distressing. I do not deny that Moss's stories were interesting; on the contrary, there was much human character in them, and his racy manner of relating them was not unamusing. But they were not at all the kind of stories that one likes to hear at the Bantocks': they were altogether out of place.

But never for a moment did the Bantocks relax their beautiful conception of hospitality. I could see that neither Mrs. Bantock nor Russell cared for Moss's stories, which, indeed, were absolutely unrefined, and when he was not looking at them, they seemed weary and even disgusted; as soon, however, as he looked at them, they smiled brightly and leaned forward with interest. Mr. Bantock, as usual, said very little, but his accustomed smile of benevolence never failed. Moss went on and on. Some of his stories were really coarse, and sometimes I perceived, with a momentary horror, that he was on the verge of a word for which there could be no excuse; however, he always saved himself in that respect. "I know what's due to ladies," he said afterwards, with unconscious irony. My fear that he might, at any moment, go too far was a strain on me, and several times I endeavoured to change the conversation, when, to my surprise, not only Cousin Charlotte, but Mrs. Bantock refused to notice me; it was, no doubt, another instance of her kindly tolerance of Moss. Indeed, so far did she go in this direction that I heard her say to Cousin Charlotte, outside the door: "My dear Charlotte, I'm very much obliged to you!" She even thanked her persecutor!

Cousin Charlotte departed two days later, but Moss stayed for a week. I thought, when she left, that he would resume his more fitting demeanour. But Moss, having got his head as it were, kept it. He rattled away, cutting jokes, and going so far as to chaff Mr. Bantock, who bore it smilingly, though he did not reply. In fact, nobody could ever think of anything appropriate to say to him except Tom, and Tom, I am sorry to say, descended to his level and returned him joke for joke. He professed to like Moss, but he treated him without any respect, whereas the others were always carefully polite to him. Tom called Moss "Ikey," which, I am told, is a sportive variant of Isaac, Moss's Christian name. Oddly enough, Tom was the only member of the Bantock family for whom Moss has subsequently professed any regard. He has asked Tom to dinner several times.

But to the other Bantocks he has shown an extraordinary, almost a wicked, ingratitude. It is true that he enabled Mr. Bantock and Russell to make a few thousand pounds in connection with a Company, and that he sent Mrs. Bantock a small nugget of gold. But that was a very small return — his opportunities considered — for their kindness and hospitality. Virtue is its own reward, but one does expect (as Mrs. Bantock said to me in confidence) some little gratitude from people. Moss has been associating with people who have titles and so forth — as Russell says, one hardly knows which to despise the most, Moss's snobbishness or their sordid encouragement of him — and he has completely dropped the Bantocks. It is an absurd phrase to use of Moss, but it expresses the fact. Nevertheless, the Bantocks speak of him with very little bitterness. Mrs. Bantock sometimes refers with much humour to the trial of having him in the house, and Russell says it is foolish to be kind to cads like Moss. That is all.

VIII

THE TRAGEDY OF THE HAMPER

UNDER all her trials, only twice or thrice have I known Mrs. Bantock fail to retain complete control of her naturally spirited, but patiently schooled temper; only once have I known her administer a physical rebuke. It is a bitter memory of my life that of this unique event I myself was the unhappy cause.

In spite of Mrs. Bantock's beautifully robust appearance, she has told me that she does not enjoy absolutely perfect health. She has to be extremely careful. It is imperative that she should have nine hours' sleep and a certain amount of gentle exercise every day. And, above all, her doctor insists that it is absolutely necessary for her to have a generous and nourishing diet. She is indifferent to material things (as one would expect from her lofty principles and spiritual nature), and she does not care what she eats, but her doctor gives emphatic orders that her food must be elaborate, to tempt her appetite, and perfectly cooked, and that she must take it at strictly regular hours. Her tea and toast at half-past eight, her substantial breakfast at nine, her sandwiches at twelve, her lunch of several courses at two, her tea with something solid at five, her dinner (one of the very best in London) at a quarter to eight, and her light and wholesome supper at eleven, are all part of a carefully thought-out and rigorous treatment. As a consequence, meals are a solemn occasion in the Bantock family, and theirs is the most punctual house I know. Mrs. Bantock does not mind anticipating the due time of a meal, as when she has to dine earlier than usual to go to the theatre, but to have one later than usual is injurious and even dangerous to her system. So far as it is possible, again, she has to avoid dining, or even lunching, at houses where it is not certain the food will be unexceptionable. All this, as she assures me, is a great nuisance to her; she hates to be troubled with such trifles, and would be thankful enough for a crust and a glass of water. The doctor, however, is adamant on the subject. I have to make this matter clear, that the gravity of the lamentable event I am going to record may be properly appreciated.

The Bantocks took a house in Scotland one summer, and hospitably asked me to stay a fortnight with them. At that time Ethel Bantock had a fancy to learn Latin, and I was glad to be of some assistance to her in the task. Well, one morning, I was looking over an exercise she had written, the other men being out fishing, when Mrs. Bantock entered the library. She said she had just remembered a promise to go and lunch with Mrs. Dunlop, a neighbour, and Ethel was to come with her. Ethel begged to be excused; she had a headache, and disliked Mrs. Dunlop. Mrs. Bantock said somebody must go; she hated driving alone, and besides, the coachman being the only available man-servant, somebody must go to open gates. Ethel suggested that I should go, and finally I had the honour to be chosen.

Now, the Dunlops' place was a two hours' drive away, over a sparsely inhabited and rather desolate country. Something had happened to the open carriage, and, the day being extremely hot, we went in a one-horse waggonette, since the brougham was too stuffy. There were three of us, Mrs. Bantock, the coachman, and I. We started about twelve o'clock, and all went well for half the distance. Mrs. Bantock had taken a novel

d, but the road was too rough, and
:casionally spoke to me; she was in
:rful mood, and I enjoyed the drive
nuch. But when we had gone for
an hour, the horse fell suddenly
— dead lame — and could not go
Mrs. Bantock rated the coachman
ly, as he deserved, and enquired
was to be done. The coachman was
inion that the horse could not drag
pad, even at a walk, without injury
elf, and it was a valuable animal.
, gradually, the whole horror of the
on came upon us. It was a deso-
ountry, as I have said. There was
house anywhere near. It was one
k. For Mrs. Bantock to walk seven
ht miles on a hot day was out of the
on. But before the coachman or
ld go back to the house, or on to
'unlops', procure a fresh conveyance,
it back, and Mrs. Bantock could be
·ht finallv to one or the other house,

it would be nearly four o'clock, half-past three at the earliest, even if she were to walk until she was met. And the doctor had ordered her — the idea of ordering Mrs. Bantock seems a paradox, almost indecent, but it is the usual phrase — never, on any account, to lunch a minute later than two o'clock! Mrs. Bantock and I looked at each other: blank impotence was on our faces.

"We shall starve!" said Mrs. Bantock. It was characteristic of her kindly nature that she included me in the visitation, though, in fact, my anxiety was entirely on her account. The tragic sentence fell passionately on the air; I had no reply.

The coachman suggested that the best course would be for him to lead the horse and the waggonette back to the house, and return as quickly as possible with the pony-chaise. I think he was glad to go; Mrs. Bantock had rebuked him with some severity. So he went, with orders that lunch was to be kept, and I remained in attendance on his mistress. It is remarkable that she wasted no idle words in lamentation or regret; with a face of calm though bitter resolution she walked, her novel in her hand, to the little wood which was beside the road. Fortunately, the root of a tree made a natural seat on which, with the help of the carriage rug, it was found possible to make her tolerably comfortable. I sat on the ground at her feet, and watched the waggonette till it had passed out of sight down the hill. She began to read in silence. I felt very awkward, I confess; consolation was impossible, and I could think of nothing to say. But presently an idea occurred to me, one of those flashes which light a gloomy situation as the lightning a murky landscape. I remembered that from the road, some two miles back, I had seen a prosperous-looking farmhouse. Surely it would be possible to procure some food there! At once I mentioned the idea to Mrs. Bantock. Her equanimity had been greatly tried, and she seemed to be angry with me for not having thought of it before — I know it was a very stupid lapse on my part. However, "Go at once," she said; "bring any thing they've got that's eatable. Make haste!" And then, with the thoughtfulness for others which never deserts her, she added: "I'm so glad you'll get some lunch, after all." Not a thought for herself!

I started at a brisk walk, and she called after me, "Hurry!" in that authoritative tone which no wise person ever resists. I broke into a run down the hill. It was a very hot day, the sun was quite malignant, but, in my zeal, I think I must have done those two miles and a half in half an hour. I arrived at the farm, fatigued and in a disgusting state of heat, and, after some difficulty with a couple of sheep-

ucceeded in knocking at the door.
ıately, the farmer's wife was at home,
oved herself a kind and sympathetic
. She was well provided with food.
was a cold chicken in the house,
this she made some pleasant-look-
ındwiches; she added two hard-
eggs, some cut bread and butter,
›me shortbread. So far, excellent.
uestion of drink raised a difficulty,
er. The doctor, I knew, had or-
Mrs. Bantock to drink champagne
ch, but, of course, that could not be
The farmer's wife had milk, beer,
'hiskey — that was all. Finally, I
d to take a bottle of milk and some
ey-and-water in a bottle, the latter
e Mrs. Bantock, after the trouble
ad gone, and was going, through,
wish for a stimulant, even of that
kind, in the absence of any other.
ottles were packed on the top of the
n a little hamper, which was care-

fully tied with string, and, with an injunction from the farmer's wife to handle it with caution, I set out on my return journey.

It was not an agreeable journey. The sun, as I have said, was blazing, the road was dusty and chiefly up-hill, the hamper was heavy and extremely awkward to carry. I was stimulated by the thought that, if I made great haste, Mrs. Bantock might yet have some lunch not long after her usual time, so I made what haste I could, running whenever there was an interval of down-hill, but I confess that in my weakness I almost cursed the day that I was born. For one moment I was tempted to think that the trial was mine rather than Mrs. Bantock's, but I remembered, in shame, the greater delicacy of her frame and the danger to her system, and hurried on. Presently I entertained the idiotic idea that I might make a short cut across country, and diverged from the road. Three misadventures punished the folly. The first was unimportant, — a mere scare from another couple of sheep-dogs. The other two were more serious, and, indeed, one or both of them must have caused the horrible catastrophe to which my narrative is hurrying. I had to scale a low stone wall; I balanced the hamper on the top, but, as I swung over, my foot caught it, and it rolled with me to the ground. Further on, I had to jump a stream; I slipped on the further side, and fell headlong, the hamper striking against a stone. Breathlessly, I picked it up, and hurried on. I panted, I stumbled, but on, on I hurried, regained the road, and felt with joy I must be near the goal.

At length, covered with mud and dust and perspiration, I reached the brow of the hill, and was refreshed by the sight of Mrs. Bantock, leaning back against the tree and reading her novel; she looked very cool and comfortable. When she saw me, she took off her gloves in preparation for the lunch, and graciously came a step or two to meet me. At first, she rebuked my slowness, but her vein of humour never deserts her, even in the keenest trial, and when she saw my dreadful state, flushed, fiery-red as I was, and with my knickerbockers and stockings a mass of oozy mud from the stream, she laughed heartily and good-humouredly at my plight. She asked me what I had got; and when I told her, "Oh, come," she said, "that's capital!" and, again not thinking of herself, she added: "I'm so glad — I was afraid you'd feel the want of lunch — you're a splendid forager!" Gratified by the compliment, I placed the hamper on the root of the tree, undid the string, and opened the lid.

I can hardly bear to tell you what I saw. So long as I live, waking or sleeping, it will haunt me. Both bottles were broken; sandwiches, eggs, bread and butter, shortbread, everything was saturated with milk and whiskey-and-water. There was a terrible silence. I did not dare to look Mrs. Bantock in the face; nervously I watched her action as she took up a sandwich, looked at it, smelt it, and threw it back in the basket. She did not speak, but in a moment I had received the severest slap on the face and ear that I remember.

What is a slap on the face? It is nothing, and surely an offender should be glad if he may — by so quickly ended a punishment — so purge his offence. Besides, it argued some intimacy between us. I am sure Mrs. Bantock would not have slapped me if she had not regarded me as a friend. But for a second my only idea was the pain; it hurt very much. The remembrance flashed through my brain that Mrs. Bantock, as a girl, had done gymnastics; her arm was strong; she wore many rings, and they, in particular, hurt me. We stood in silence another moment. I took a fleeting glance at Mrs. Bantock; she was slightly flushed, and was looking again into the hamper. The tension was terrible; I almost wished that she would slap me again to break it.

Presently she spoke: "If it had only been the milk! I think I could have eaten them. But whiskey — did n't you know that I loathe whiskey? I suppose you brought it for yourself." The reproach was a little cruel and unmerited, but I did not dare to reply to it. I stammered apologies for my carelessness. Mrs. Bantock did not reply to them, but presently, with an effort of which few men and women would have been capable, she recovered her philosophic calm. "Take that thing away," she said. I removed the hamper, and she sat down on the root again, and resumed her novel. It was wonderful to see such resignation.

But I was horribly nervous. I did not dare to speak; I did not know what to do. I stood foolishly, and soon she looked up and said: "You may as well sit down." It was a kind thought; I sat down on the grass. At that time I would have given the world for something to distract my thoughts; a popular novel would have been a priceless boon. Time passed on leaden feet. At length, after what seemed a year, the pony-chaise arrived, and Mrs. Bantock rose, still in silence. There was room only for two in it, and the coachman was wanted to look after the lame horse at the house. So I had to walk, Mrs. Bantock kindly expressing regret at the circumstance. I left the hamper—cursing it, I am afraid, in my heart—at the farm on the way, and reached the house about five o'clock, footsore, and with a heart most sore as well; I did not know if I was still in disgrace.

On this point, my friend, with her angelic kindness, soon relieved me. I ate some cold meat in the dining-room, and, too sad to go into the drawing-room where I heard voices, I went to the deserted library, and sat with my face buried in my hands. Presently, some one entered; I looked up, and Mrs. Bantock stood before me, smiling a sweet smile of forgiveness. Her first words were kind and reassuring. "I'm afraid you must be dreadfully tired after your walk," she said. I said it was nothing, and renewed my apologies about the hamper. So entirely had she overcome her just resentment that she laughed. "Of course," she said, "I was in fun when I pretended to be angry." With such admirable tact she spared my feelings, and never once did she allude to the hamper again. Hers is the goodness which not only forgives, but forgets.

IX

ETHEL'S SOCIALISM

I THINK that Carlyle would have admired Mr. Bantock very much. A strong, silent man Carlyle would have called him. In fact, Mr. Bantock very seldom says anything. He is content to do his work in the world, from eleven till four every day, with only an hour's interval for lunch — excepting a week now and then, and two months in the summer when he takes his well-earned rest. Evèn in his relaxations, at whist or golf, he indulges in no speech beÿond an occasional exclamation. He says little at his own table, though he is sometimes prone, as I have said — with the object of encouraging poor men like myself — to enlarge on his early struggles. Some time ago, however, fate compelled him frequently to argue and, finally, to make something like a speech.

I have mentioned that Ethel Bantock was at one time desirous to learn Latin. It was a sign of an enquiring mind, and she displayed that quality in other direc-tions. Now, an enquiring mind is an excellent thing in its way, and I wish to give Ethel every credit for hers, but it is apt, in youth, before it is corrected by knowledge and wisdom, to lead its pos-sessor into false conclusions. I have also mentioned that, at an earlier stage, she was attracted by the terribly unconven-tional Miss Clavering. This showed candour and breadth of view, which, again, are excellent characteristics when properly directed, though always a little dangerous. I have reminded you of these things to soften the shock, if possible, when I tell you that, at the age of sixteen, Ethel declared herself a convinced Socialist. She contrived to get and read most pernicious books on the subject. She delivered herself of theories about wealth of which the logical upshot would have been that the Bantocks should divest themselves of theirs. She found out the number of hours during which omnibus-conductors and people of that sort work every day, and reproached Russell, and, by implication, her own father, for not working so much. She hinted that poor Tom, who did no work, ought to starve. She found out what the cottagers in the country had to eat, and instituted ridiculous comparisons between that and the food consumed in her own house. I remember that she once, taking up the menu, at dinner, complained indignantly of there being eight courses. Unfortunately for her, Mrs. Bantock was present, and said at once that if she heard any more of that, Ethel should be put on a cottager's diet and not appear in the dining-room,—a threat which quenched her zeal for equality in that direction. Mrs. Bantock sensibly remarked that cottagers neither needed nor could appreciate such cooking as was absolutely necessary for herself.

In her mother's presence, indeed, Ethel did not dare to ventilate her theories. She tried to do so only twice: once on the occasion I have mentioned, and once when she said she wished half the money spent on her dress to be given to the poor. On this latter occasion, Mrs. Bantock told her to leave the room, since she would not leave off arguing. But one summer, when I was staying in the country, Mrs. Bantock had to go away for a week on an errand of kindness and pity: to nurse her aunt, a very rich and (I am sure) a most excellent old lady. Then Ethel had a clear field and made a most unscrupulous use of it. Mr. Bantock is devoted to his children, and, perhaps, too tolerant of their very few and transitory faults. He was quite unable in this case to adopt his wife's kind but unflinching firmness. He began to argue. Now, this was a most unwise step, because, like many most sagacious minds, Mr. Bantock's is somewhat slow in its working, whereas Ethel is nimble-witted. So that, although her arguments were absurd, and Mr. Bantock's sound and well established, Ethel invariably had the last word and an illusory appearance of victory. At first I endeavoured to assist my host, but Ethel turned on me with such rudeness — I might almost say with such savagery — that I was reduced to silence — dignified, I trust.

"Oh, *you!*" she said, — "you dare n't call your soul your own. You 're a born slave. So long as you 're comfortable, you don't care what injustice is done in the world."

" I beg your pardon," I said; " I care very much."

" Nonsense. You 've no spirit at all. Look at the way you fall flat on your face when mother bullies you."

I said I thought it was a privilege to be criticised by Mrs. Bantock.

"That 's humbug," she returned. "You 'd say it was a privilege if she were to box your ears." I remembered the incident of the hamper and was silent. It would have been useless to try to explain my point of view to Ethel. She went on: " It 's because you 're cowardly and lazy. You care for nothing but being comfortable. *You* need n't talk. But look here, father, don't you see — " and so on. Of course, after this I preferred to intervene infrequently. Russell was away on a visit. Tom gave his father no assistance, and, in fact, seemed to enjoy his perplexity. I am afraid that Mr. Bantock, who usually liked his meals, found them an absolute torment during this week.

Ethel returned to the sordid subject of food, and insisted on the inequality between that of the Bantocks and that of the surrounding cottagers. In vain Mr. Bantock pointed out that brain-workers required a more nourishing diet. Ethel laughed this argument to scorn, even going so far as to hint a disbelief in her family's brain-work. She went on to say that if brain-work was the consideration, then great geniuses ought to fare better than bankers and brewers, whereas the reverse was notoriously the case. It seemed to her to be shocking that people who produced great works of art should be so ill-paid. Literary people, too, were shamefully treated. I rather agreed with this last remark and sighed sympathetically; but Ethel did not welcome my sympathy.

"Oh," she said, "I don't mean you and

your silly, rotten writings; I'm sure you get quite as much as they deserve. I mean people who write really great things, — things that make the world better."

Mr. Bantock said that, to his certain knowledge, a popular novelist who banked with him made five thousand a year, and he had heard of a woman who got a thousand a year by writing an article on Fashion once a week. Ethel was quite angry, and said excitedly that she did not mean those people either. "Milton," she said, "only got ten pounds for 'Paradise Lost,'" and to the remark that Milton died a long time ago, she replied that she did not believe he would have got much more now. It was monstrous, she said, that great poets should be in want while people like themselves lived in luxury. Then Mr. Bantock pulled himself together to reply.

"My dear child," he said mildly, "the pecuniary recompense given by the community to anybody is in proportion to his usefulness. Your great poets are all very well, but they are not *useful*; they don't increase the prosperity of a country. I have no objection to them, I assure you, —none whatever; but it is absurd to suppose that they ought to be paid large incomes like people who do the work of the world."

"Such as successful music-hall singers?" Ethel forcibly interrupted.

Mr. Bantock continued with great patience: "It's impossible to argue with you if you make absurd interruptions. Of course I mean people who are really necessary to the world. You see I'm arguing on your own lines. I say nothing of the rights of property, without which the world could not last for a single minute."

"Well, but take your case, father: how are you necessary to the world?"

"I take care of its money."

"Yes; but ought you to get, for that, twice as much in a week as a clever writer would make in a year,—a really clever writer? And three times as much a year as a Cabinet Minister?—not that I think much of them."

"Well, part of our income is your mother's."

"That 's beer," said Ethel, contemptuously, forgetting altogether Waterloo and Trafalgar.

"And a very good thing, too," Mr. Bantock replied with good-humour.

"But mother does n't make the beer," Ethel said,—an irreverence of thought which, I confess, shocked me.

"Ah, there," said Mr. Bantock, "you touch on private property. I can't argue that with you."

"Why not?"

"Because it 's self-evident."

"I don't see it. Won't you argue it, father?"

"No," said Mr. Bantock, firmly, "I will not."

Ethel looked as though she had won. I confess I was inclined to blame Mr. Bantock for allowing these discussions at all; it was an amiable weakness, but a weakness still. They went on at least twice a day, and since Ethel would not let me speak, I found them tedious. But Mr. Bantock never really put his foot down until the evening before Mrs. Bantock was to return. Ethel, no doubt aware that her reign of argument would be at an end the next day, had collected all her forces for a field-day, and, as ill-luck would have it, the morning's paper gave her a superficially good ground for manœuvres. Some years before, Mr. Bantock, with the open-handed generosity natural to him, had advanced six hundred pounds to the inventor (a young man whom he wished to help) of a new kind of soda-water bottle stopper, to work the patent, on condition of receiving half the profits of the venture. It had turned out a great success, and for some time Mr. Bantock had drawn between three and four thousand a year from it. The affair was then turned into a company, and Mr. Bantock, fearing that the invention might at any time be superseded by another, disposed of his interest in it for (I think) thirty thousand pounds, — a respectable sum, but one which Mr. Bantock would not have thought worth while mentioning as a special cause for gratulation. But that morning's paper contained the prospectus of the new company. Ethel saw it, and, remembering the invention, put several apparently innocent questions to her father at lunch, which he, pathetically unsuspicious, answered frankly and in good faith. Ethel seemed thoughtful, and at dinner she opened fire.

"I don't quite understand, father," she said, still with seeming innocence, "about this company: you are to get thirty thousand pounds, are n't you?"

Mr. Bantock replied in the affirmative, simply and even a little complacently. He little knew what was to follow!

"Why do you get that?"

"Because I invested in the thing originally."

"Let's see," said Ethel, quite impertinently judicial, "that was six hundred pounds, was n't it?"

Mr. Bantock seemed to have a dim idea of her drift, an application of some absurd notion about unearned increment. "Yes, that was it," he said, "but of course I might have lost it all. It was a speculation."

"Is that the same as gambling?" Ethel asked.

Mr. Bantock answered, with a little natural irritation: "No, of course not; quite a different thing."

Ethel ejaculated: "Thirty thousand pounds!"

"Well," said her father, "if I had n't advanced the six hundred, there'd be no money for anybody. You don't understand. I ran the risk of losing it."

"But thirty thousand pounds! Fifty times as much as you put in, and all in six years! It does seem unfair. Without any work!"

"My dear child, you don't understand economical questions. Without brains and directing powers, no amount of work is any good—"

"But *you* did n't direct—*your* brains did n't come in at all—"

"My capital did, and that's the same thing—the same thing precisely."

"Then the whole system's wrong. I call it infamous. If I were you, I could n't touch this money."

At last Mr. Bantock's patience gave way. He had borne much, but he could bear no more. To hear his own child attack the most sacred institutions of human society, and to stigmatise his accidentally profitable, but originally generous, action as infamous! He was a silent man, but now his duty compelled him to make a little speech. He raised his voice, almost shouted, in fact.

"Be silent, Ethel! Not one word more! I never heard such monstrous ideas, never. If your dear mother had been here, you would not have dared. Where you get them from I can't imagine; if there are any books of that sort in my house, they ought to be burnt. As for what you say, I suppose argument's wasted on you, but I'll explain, once for all. It's such men as me, with capital and foresight, who make progress and prosperity possible. To deny it is to be false to all the principles you have ever been taught. The whole Constitution, the Monarchy itself, depend on it. I will not hear another word. What you say is simply contrary to Christianity. I shall inform your mother of what you say."

Ethel had looked down at her plate, but when he had finished his admirable little oration, she looked up and met my eyes. I could not help being amused at her discomfiture — so necessary for her good — and was smiling, and I regret to say she was angry for days and took every opportunity of annoying me. Tom said, "Hear, hear!" after Mr. Bantock's remarks, flippantly, I could not help thinking.

The next day, when Mrs. Bantock returned, Ethel's socialistic books were solemnly burnt in the library. It was an impressive spectacle, and Mrs. Bantock's observations were trenchant and memorable. Ethel never openly talked socialism again, and Mr. Bantock was able to return to his usual silence. He had spoken, when duty compelled him, to the point, and, having spoken, dismissed the matter from his mind with the ease of which strong natures, who do not speak, but act, alone are capable. I wish Carlyle had met him.

X

THE ATHLETIC SPORTS

IT was a few days later in the same summer in which Mr. Bantock was so sorely tried by Ethel's socialism, when a girl friend of Ethel's, a "pal," as she rather vulgarly called her, came to stay in the house, and, at the same time, an Oxford chum of Tom's. I was still staying there, being useful, I am glad to say, in arranging the accounts and drawing up the annual report of one of Mrs. Bantock's excellent charities. Both friends were young people of extremely good connections, and I am sure that Mrs. Bantock was glad to make the house more lively for her dear children. But, really, their high spirits were excessive. They organised all sorts of games and romps, in which Russell and I had occasionally to join, though greatly disliking such amusements; he, I think, even more than I, even as his dignity is greater than mine. For example, I remember with pain how he was induced to sit on a bottle (laid on its side) one evening, and endeavour to light a candle while in that position. Twice he rolled off on to the floor, amid the unfeeling laughter of his tormentors, and when, finally, he rose (not, by the way, having accomplished the silly feat), his face was white with passion, though, with a noble effort, he suppressed it. They suggested that Russell and I, in imitation of Tom and his friend, should sit blindfold on the floor, and hit at each other with rolled-up newspapers, but this we absolutely refused to do. They succeeded, however, in persuading me to lie with my head resting on the edge of a chair, and my feet on another, and, so situated, to attempt the useless task of drawing a chair from underneath me and passing it back, over my body, into its original position. Of course, I fell heavily on the floor, and everybody laughed as though it were something amusing. I thought of the phrase "butchered to make a Roman holiday."

These things used to happen in the drawing-room after dinner, and the comfort of the rest of us was sacrificed to the hilarity of the abnormally vivacious quartette, — Tom and Ethel and their two friends. Mrs. Bantock, who, I knew, disapproved, was assured by Ethel's friend that they always did these things at the house of her mother, — the first cousin, by the way, of a duke, — and so it was decided not to interfere with the child's home pleasures. But they were a nuisance, to be frank, and I am sorry to say that the disturbance did not end here.

Practical jokes were played on Russell and me, and even on Mr. Bantock, to the extent of causing Russell to forget his habitual correctness and indulge in profane language, and Mr. Bantock to break through his accustomed silence. Tobogganing on tea trays down the stairs was a frequent incident, until it was stopped by Mrs. Bantock's tripping on a tray somebody left on a landing, and very nearly — I shudder to recall it. There was no end to the annoyances.

An unamiable characteristic of these young people was that they were for ever quarrelling. They were in fun, of course; still it was an ugly thing to pretend, and the licence of invective they permitted themselves was really shocking. When they indulged in their really vulgar adjectives and monstrous charges against one another, Mrs. Bantock used to smile and say, "Foolish children!" but I am sure she was distressed. They tried to drag Russell into these quarrels, and even went so far that he privately intimated to Tom that the next time it happened he would go away; and Tom, corrupted, as it were, by evil communications, told the others, and Russell was treated with an exaggerated reverence quite as bad as the former flippancy.

But I pass over the minor inconveniences caused by the presence of these young friends, and go on to the athletic sports of which it was the direct cause.

When I went, one afternoon, into the drawing-room, at tea-time, I was greeted with a noisy question from Tom, "I say, can you climb the greasy pole?" My head was a little dazed with adding up figures all the afternoon, and for a moment I could not remember in what business that disgusting implement was used. "Silence gives consent," said Tom; "that's splendid; I expect you'll win the prize. Any good at an obstacle race?" I then learned that at the Dessents', where Tom, Ethel, and their friends had been lunching, there had been discussed a project for some athletic sports. Mrs. Bantock said she thought it a nice idea. "I suppose the villagers will run races," she said, "quite like the olden times." "Oh, no," Tom answered, "it's for us. There's the Dessents, us, the Masters, the Duntons — everybody's going to be asked. We shall have big fields. The whole thing's going to be done properly. Running, jumping, obstacle races, the pole, donkey races, — without saddle and bridle, you know, — the whole thing. It was Frank's idea" — Frank was his friend — "and the Dessents caught on splendidly. I said we'd do it here." — "I'm afraid that would not be convenient," Mrs. Bantock interjected. — "Oh, you need n't be alarmed; the Dessents insisted, and they've got a bigger field than we have. They're going to do it in style. Sir Edgar is going up to town to-morrow to get the prizes. I say, Russell, shall we practise donkey-riding —there is a donkey, is n't there?—after tea?" And so forth. Nothing else but these wretched sports was talked about for the rest of the day. When I heard that they were the idea of Tom's friend, I had a gloomy foreboding that some inconvenience or even disaster would ensue, and the next day strengthened me in this view.

Lady Dessent came over in the afternoon. She is a little, vivacious woman, and though her eldest child is nineteen, I have seen her romp with young people like one of themselves. She is very good-natured, I believe, and is extremely popular in the county, both in her own class and among the people, but I think Mrs. Bantock does not like her, perhaps detecting in her a want of reverence for the really solemn things of life. She came over, and at once began to talk about the athletic sports with an enthusiasm which, at her age, might surely have been reserved for more important matters. "It's all arranged," she said gleefully, as though it were a matter of profound congratulation. "Edgar says he's going to make a job of it." Sir Edgar is her husband, a physically strong, jovial, and sporting man, lacking (I am bound to say) in decorum among his friends. She went on: "He's already set the men to work putting up hurdles, and given orders for the pole, and now he's gone to town to get the prizes. We expect everybody to go in for everything—within limits, of course; we can't expect you to jump hurdles." She looked at Mrs. Bantock as she spoke, and laughed, quite unconscious of the utter want of taste in the remark. But Mrs. Bantock only smiled, and Lady Dessent went on: "Edgar's remembered some more races and things since your children came over. One 's the husband and wife race: did you ever hear of it? Well, the husband goes down on the ground and the wife takes hold of his ankles and then he goes along on his hands as quickly as he can. Edgar and I are going to practise to-morrow." She had been looking at Mrs. Bantock, and suddenly she turned away her head; her eyes met Tom's, who was looking at her with a grin. Tom suddenly rose and left the room. Lady Dessent was silent for a few minutes, and the others talked. Presently Ethel said, "Where 's Tom?" and went to find him, and she not returning, Mrs. Bantock sent me to bring them back, as some details of the sports were being considered.

I was astonished when I reached the hall. Ethel was leaning against a chest, the tears running down her face, and Tom, his handkerchief stuffed into his mouth, was stamping furiously about the hall. I stood amazed. Then Tom took out the handkerchief, threw back his head, and emitted a horrible shouting noise, which no doubt was meant for laughter, but was not at all the way in which nice people laugh. "Oh, Lord!" he cried. "Fancy the governor going along on his hands and the mater holding up his feet! I should die!" His sister, I am sorry to say, seemed to share his offensive merriment to the point of speechlessness. It is difficult to excuse their conduct, but I fancy the explanation is this: great reverence, such as I am sure both Ethel and Tom had for their parents, has been often found (in the mediæval church, for example) to be attended by periods of short, but absolute, reaction. Perhaps to live always with a man of such absolute propriety and dignity as Mr. Bantock, and so perfect a woman as Mrs. Bantock, does overstrain the faculty of the mind for veneration, and a temporary reaction sets in, though

I am certain I should never find it so in my own case. But it was in every way a painful spectacle. I told them briefly that they were to go to the drawing-room. "I say," said Tom, "for heaven's sake don't tell what we were laughing at," and Ethel, still apparently unable to speak, menaced me foolishly with her clenched hand. I replied coldly that I would not; that, indeed, I could see nothing amusing in the suggestion, but my coldness had the effect only of producing another ribald explosion. Tom said he would not go back. "If I looked at them, I should yell!" So Ethel returned with me alone. When Lady Dessent went, Tom was in the hall and said to her: "I say, Lady Dessent, if we could persuade them —" He glanced back at the drawing-room, indicating his parents, beyond doubt. Lady Dessent positively laughed, and I have never been able to like her since.

Well, the day arrived. The young people chattered about it all the morning and at lunch, until the rest of us were quite weary. In the afternoon, we all drove over to the Dessents'. Russell, I thought, looked a trifle uneasy, but Mr. and Mrs. Bantock had no foreboding of anything but a rather tedious amusement, — an unconsciousness which I remembered afterwards as strangely pathetic. There were seats all along one side of the field, and everybody in the neighbourhood was there. All the first "events," running and jumping, were comparatively innocuous: it was possible to leave off running after going a short distance, and give up in humorous despair, and one was soon out of the jumping competitions. But the last half of the programme was something like torture. The obstacle race! I got myself involved in the meshes of a horrible net, while everybody mocked me, as might savages some trapped enemy. Poor Russell, who was in a suit of nice clean flannels, came to grief over a diabolical water-jump, and was splashed from head to foot. I was thrown by a donkey, and narrowly escaped the infuriated brute's hoofs, Tom having struck it hard with a heartless disregard of the dumb animal's feelings. There was actually a greasy pole, and the chivalrous Russell, unable to resist Lady Dessent's pleading, completed on it the ruin of his flannels.

But these, after all, are minor matters. The great catastrophe was caused by Mr. Bantock's unexpected conduct. There was a noble humility in the idea, at which he ultimately arrived, that he ought to throw himself heartily into the spirit of these abominable sports. For most of the time he had sat a decorous spectator, but at last Lady Dessent, by incessant entreaties and feminine wiles, worked him into taking an active part. You will think that nothing short of temporary madness can account for his subsequent conduct, but I am convinced that he was possessed of an honest desire to please. His judgment went wrong, and that is all; we are none of us infallible. Still, it was a long time before my respect for Mr. Bantock was absolutely restored. I experienced that cruel sorrow, the injury of a cherished ideal.

The horrible "husband and wife" race came on. I was standing near Mrs. Bantock, and Mr. Bantock approached, egged on by Lady Dessent. "Come, Flora," he said, "it's our turn; let's show them we're not too old to win a prize." The scene seemed to whirl round, and indistinctly I heard the almost parricidal sound of Tom's and Ethel's applause. Mrs. Bantock's astonished, but resolute tones recalled me. "My *dear* Charles," she said, "what *do* you mean?" "Oh, *do* come into it, Mrs. Bantock," Lady Dessent interposed; "you *must* go in for something." Mrs. Bantock firmly, but good-humouredly, declined. Then a monstrous thing happened. Mr. Bantock positively caught hold of her hands and raised her to her feet. "Come on," he said. She answered, still with wonderful control of herself, "If you insist on making an exhibition of yourself, I'll watch, but I won't join you." And then, incautiously, perhaps to dissuade him still, she walked with him to the spot where the other competitors were standing. The men lay down in the grass, like reptiles, and kicked up their legs for the women to seize. Actually, Mr. Bantock — you remember I have described him as a man of great dignity, and somewhat stout — did the same. Then, at last, Mrs. Bantock turned and walked back to her seat;

her mien was noble, but what she must have suffered!

I hesitate to harrow your feelings further, but I must mention the sack race. Mr. Bantock, not dependent in this on his wife's assistance, got into a sack. Russell and I were not in this "heat," and stood side by side watching the proceedings, horribly fascinated. Mr. Bantock distanced his competitors, and was coming in first, when he fell. Surely that was humiliation enough? No: he rolled over and over till he reached the post. I glanced at Russell. He looked sick with shame. . . .

The sports were over at last and we drove home, Mr. Bantock still gay and making much of a prize he had won in the sack race degradation. I fancy that Mrs. Bantock took an opportunity to explain to him how far he had lapsed from the path of his habitual dignity, for he was more silent than usual at dinner.

Mrs. Bantock turned the conversation away from the sports. But evidently she bore no malice. To the end of their fatal visit, she was kind and affectionate to her children's friends.

XI

MRS. BANTOCK'S PORTRAIT

As a family, the Bantocks are not u
terested in matters of literature and
though they are of opinion that t
should be kept in their proper p
subordinate to the real interests of
The word "art," by the way, conn
in their conversation pictures and sta
only, and literature, everything pri
in the form of a book. Both Mr.
Mrs. Bantock extend some patronag
the latter; he is a student of the T
and she reads a good many novels,

they have not read. Mr. Bantock takes his views, more or less, from his favourite journal, and Mrs. Bantock from hers, which I will not name for fear of exciting envy; but they both argue that, after all, the great public is the only judge, and its judgment can be inferred only from the prosperity or pecuniary failure of those who seek it. It stands to reason, Mr. Bantock says, that if a man understands his business, he makes money by it, and, remembering that literature is at its best a poor trade, he has a considerable respect for men who can make even three or four thousand a year at it: he admits that in a more profitable calling they might have made substantial incomes. As for people who are content to work hard for the miserable sum which is the average remuneration of literature, he confesses that he regards them with mistrust, but he says generously that, after all, it is their own affair.

These opinions considered, it may be thought that literature would not have troubled the peaceful lives of the Bantocks. On the contrary, it has been, at times, a veritable nuisance to them. There was, for example, the case of Ethel's dreadful books on socialism. But they suffered more acutely at the time, a few years ago, when there seemed to be — one can hardly believe it now — quite a craze for books which contained improper incidents or allusions. It was impossible to prevent these books penetrating into Grosvenor Place: the authorities at the library, who might have stopped them, were (in Mrs. Bantock's opinion) extraordinarily lax. Her own principle in the matter was comprehensive. "Of course," she said, "there are dreadful people in the world, but no refined person, certainly no woman, ought to know anything about them." Consequently, when, every now and then, in reading some innocent-looking novel, she came upon a passage contrary to all nice feeling, she was very indignant. It happened once that her own child, Ethel, brought her an embarrassing question suggested by one of these books, — only once indeed, for Mrs. Bantock severely discouraged Ethel's curiosity and forbade her to read any book in future not previously read by her mother. The nuisance did not even stop at this point, for occasionally people would have the bad taste to argue about these books in her presence. Cousin Charlotte was a great offender in this way. "My dear Flora," she said once, when Mrs. Bantock had been expressing her grievance, "I haven't read the book, — I hardly ever read English fiction: it can't even be improper without being dull, — but do be fair to the poor woman: you can't restrict writers to good people, — they 're not even half the world." Mrs. Bantock was not convinced by this argument. "I see no necessity," she said, "to write about people who are not nice." "Well, but," Cousin Charlotte persisted — "Fielding and those authors?" Mrs. Bantock answered, "I have always understood that one did n't read them because they were coarse." "Poor dears!" Cousin Charlotte flippantly replied. "But Thackeray and Dickens — even they occasionally mentioned a bad person." Mrs. Bantock's consistency was unshaken. "It would have been better if they had not," she answered calmly: "besides, they did it for a good motive." "And how do you know this poor woman did n't?" "My dear Charlotte, that's absurd; the woman is full of the most dangerous ideas. It's monstrous that one should n't be able to take up a book from the library without the risk of being annoyed." I wish, by the way, that the people who attack the excellent

Mr. Mudie for his occasional censorship had heard Mrs. Bantock on the subject. But these discussions and the cause of them were a sore trial to her; literature, in fact, has had the impudence frequently to annoy Mrs. Bantock, and since she is intellectually typical (though superior to most) of those people whom in this fortunate country it exists to please, I think I have done well to point out the offence.

The art of painting, I regret to say, has annoyed the Bantocks in a more material manner. Some twenty years ago, Mr. Bantock made extensive purchases among the works of those artists who were held pre-eminent at the time, paying for them considerable sums of money. He admired the pictures, and admires them still. But, of late years, they have so often met with criticism from certain of his guests — Cousin Charlotte, of course, being again unamiably conspicuous — that he resolved, a year or two ago, to sell them and buy others on different advice. He sent them to Christie's, and I am sorry to say that hardly one of them reached a quarter of the reserve price. This occasioned some severe strictures from him on the nature of art: it was infamous, he said, that things bought in good faith should so decline in price — to put it bluntly, he felt he had been swindled. Since then he has entertained a grave mistrust of artists. He has thought, at times, of buying an old master, but some of them he has seen he held to be uninteresting, and others Mrs. Bantock (speaking in confidence) has pronounced vulgar. He entirely declines to buy contemporary pictures, for fear of such another mishap, so that his original collection keeps its place.

However, he did once make an exception, and generously determined to be a patron of art. It was decided that Mrs.

Bantock's portrait should be painted and exhibited in the Academy. The result was extremely painful. I ventured to recommend an artist of my acquaintance for this important work, and Mrs. Bantock, being assured by me that his terms were moderate and that he was a gentleman, generously consented to sit to him.

From the very first, I deeply regret to say, my friend approached his task in an entirely improper spirit. After his first interview with her he asked me what I expected he could do with such a subject. I replied that I expected he would do his admirable best to be equal to so splendid an opportunity. He laughed rudely, and made a most astounding remark: "There 's no character — nothing." Mrs. Bantock with no character! I thought he must have been drinking, but explained mildly that Mrs. Bantock had the most perfect character of any known to me. "My dear fellow," he said, "that's all very well, but that's nothing for a painter. Of course one can make a picture out of self-satisfaction, and the habit of ordering people about, but it is not interesting work." He proceeded to make most distressing comments on Mrs. Bantock's personal appearance. "Sort of commonplace good looks, *plus* fat," he said. I rose at this brutal remark, and moved towards the door, but his contemptible remarks pursued me. "One could get something out of the colour of the hair, if she'd wear it properly, and if she'd get a dress that gave a fellow a chance, but of course she won't. I wish to goodness I could get out of it—if I hadn't promised in advance, confound you, I would. She's got a beastly impertinent manner, too. Confound you!" I had given him an opportunity of distinguishing himself by painting the most excellent woman in London, and this was his gratitude! Of course, a man who approached his task in such a spirit as this could not expect to give satisfaction.

After the first visit to his studio, Mrs. Bantock refused to go there again: there were studies in it which she objected to on the ground of vulgarity, and he declined to cover them up. It was therefore arranged that he should go to Grosvenor Place for two hours, twice a week, until the picture was done. An easel was set up in the library, and I contrived always to be there, — my excuse was the rearranging and cataloguing of Mr. Bantock's books, — because, since my experience of his extraordinary attitude, I was afraid the artist might offend Mrs. Bantock. The sittings were to me simply a series of nightmares. At the first of them, he had the temerity to criticise Mrs. Bantock's attire, which she, blushing with indignation, refused to alter. He then asked her to take off her bonnet, and she declined. It was, I knew, a bonnet she had just bought and liked immensely, and she wished it to be in the picture. He made an uncalled-for gesture of despair, and proceeded to pose her, and then again he had the misfortune to hold different views from his sitter's. He wanted her to smell a rose — an extremely tiring attitude — whereas she insisted on reading a book. (He actually told me afterwards that the action was monstrously inappropriate to her face.) However, he got to work at last, and all went well for ten minutes. But then Mrs. Bantock remembered that she wished to speak to the cook, and left the room. When she was gone, he broke into a torrent of coarse invective, and only stopped it as the door opened.

I must admit that Mrs. Bantock was a restless sitter. But he ought to have remembered that she held an important position in society, and had a multitude of calls on her time. It is true, as he complained to me with unnecessary bitterness, that she had frequently to give some direction to a servant, or to write a note which was urgent, and that, four or five times, people came to see her, and she went to the drawing-room to interview them. But all this did not justify his abominable language to me. On several occasions I had the greatest difficulty in persuading him not to throw up the commission. I knew that, after all her trouble, such a wicked insult might easily make Mrs. Bantock quite ill.

At the fourth sitting, she appeared in a different bonnet. He told her that he had already half painted in the other, and would not take it out. She said, in her sweetest and kindest manner, that she was very sorry to give him extra trouble, but that this was a bonnet she had just got and liked far better than the other, and she wished it *particularly* to be in the picture. He had the bad taste to argue about it, but, of course, had finally to give way. I forgot to mention that, after the second sitting, she insisted on seeing what progress he had made, and I could see that she was disappointed. She made some suggestions for alteration, which he received courteously, but was obviously determined not to adopt. After that, he refused to let her see the picture — he used to take it away with him.

Well, at last it was so far finished that he had taken it away to put the final touches in at his studio. I received one morning two notes. One was from him. It said: "I have sent it to Grosvenor Place. It is a good likeness, so far as that goes, and I flatter myself it's a decent study of flesh. But it's a cursed ugly picture — what could I do?" The other was from Mrs. Bantock: "Come round at once and explain, if you can." That was all.

With a heart sick with anxiety, I hurried to Grosvenor Place. I was shown into the library where I found Mrs. Bantock standing near the picture, placed on a sofa. She seemed to be strangely moved. She gave me one look which made me literally tremble, and said: "Tell me frankly: did you plan this outrage with that brute?"

I looked at the picture. After all, I did not think it so very bad. Something of Mrs. Bantock's queenly demeanour had not escaped the unfortunate—I really think not malicious—artist. But I understood her emotion. The reading attitude was unlucky. It emphasised Mrs. Bantock's cheeks, which were naturally full, so that they seemed, as it were, to engulf her other features, and it made her chin seem, as it were, more double than usual. The contour of as much of her figure as was shown was certainly very full. In brief, Mrs. Bantock's majesty was somehow resolved into mere stoutness,—partly, no doubt, from the loss of the authoritative expression of her eyes. No; it was not a good picture.

I pass over Mrs. Bantock's reproaches to myself. Perhaps they were just, after all, but I had not painted the picture myself. She would hear no excuses. I tried to palliate the picture, and her only answer was: "I shall send it back at once, and I shall not let Charles pay him a single penny. If he sends it to the Academy, I shall prosecute him."

The latter question was easily settled: he was quite willing that the picture should not go to the Academy. But he insisted on being paid. A terrible trouble began. Mrs. Bantock took the matter out of her husband's hands, and flatly refused to pay, and I, who knew her, was certain she would not be shaken. At last, the artist had the brutality to threaten an action at law. This was horrible. Such a vulgar notoriety would almost kill Mrs.

Bantock: it would certainly cause her to cut me altogether. I spent sleepless nights. He would not give way: he said he had a wife and children, and could not afford to humour people's meannesses; that was atrocious, because, of course, it was the principle, not the money, for which Mrs. Bantock cared. At last, by her kindness, a solution was found. I said I should very much like to buy the picture, and she consented on condition that I kept it in my attic and showed it to nobody. Another difficulty, my want of means, she also solved by advancing me the money. I am still repaying her by instalments. I pretended that the payment was from her, and the dreadful horror was over.

Can you wonder if Mrs. Bantock does not greatly care for contemporary art? But me she has quite forgiven.

XII

CONCLUDING WORDS

I HAVE related several examples of the trials by which the peace of the beautiful Bantock life is sometimes shaken. I might relate others, but I think I have done enough to show that those greatly cherished friends of mine do not enjoy, as might be superficially supposed, unbroken ease and comfort. As I stated in the beginning, my objects in writing have been two: I have wished to console poor people like myself by pointing out how great is the mistake of supposing that people like the Bantocks have not a fair portion of human troubles, and I have wished to stimulate the same poor people to greater cheerfulness in endurance by showing them with what courage and patience the Bantocks bear their afflictions. So I bring my task to a conclusion, the more readily that the trials of the Bantocks, from affection and sympathy, have been very painful to record.

It has occurred to me that somebody may object that such trials as I have described are not really severe, but are, on the contrary, even trivial. I know that such a person may exist: let me tell him how great is his mistake.

It is true that the Bantocks are free from the commoner and coarser of human troubles. They can have no anxiety about money, and can gratify any material wish within very wide limits. As a family, they are (with the exception of Mrs. Bantock, who, as I have stated, has to take very great care of herself) of singularly robust health, and, of course, such ailments as they may have, from time to time, can be more efficaciously treated by reason of their wealth than, for example, my own. I sometimes dream of a time when, by the improvement of medical science, such people as the Bantocks, having means to change their climate at will and to adopt other expensive remedies, may prolong their beautiful and useful lives indefinitely. I might mention other coarse troubles which they are enabled to avoid or, at least, greatly to assuage. But it is useless: I insist at once, with more than one philosopher before me, that it is the little things — as people think them — that matter. If the possible doubter to whom I have referred denies that such inflictions as Cousin Charlotte, or Moss, or the ruined hamper are as severe, in reality, as the more common and obvious woes he might name, — overwork, insufficient food, and the like, — I reply that he may never have had leisure to feel such subtile disturbances. A man who has to rough it and bear with ordinary anxieties has not the finer nerves to be distressed by such things; let him, then, if he is ever inclined to grudge the Bantocks their money, remember the other side of the picture and pity their sufferings.

The Bantocks themselves, however, do not ask for pity. They are content to bear their trials simply and bravely. I sometimes think that they are too strong even to pity themselves. Certainly they seem, in a spirit of gentle modesty, to rate their own sufferings less highly than those of ordinary people. A proof is that, while they will talk freely of the former, they dislike very much to hear the latter mentioned,—their feelings are too strongly touched. Thus, when some incautious person mentions a case of extreme poverty or illness, or other sad distress, Mrs. Bantock interposes. "Oh, don't talk of those horrid things," she says; "I can't get them out of my head."

But while the Bantocks show this keen pity for the common troubles from which they are free, they are justly indignant with people who incur such things by their own imprudence. They cannot easily forgive people who live beyond their incomes; they never live beyond theirs. (I have shown how even Tom's extravagances, the failing of over-generous youth, were not lightly considered by his parents.) They cannot forgive debts. I used at one time to relate to them experiences of county-court officials, sent to collect my own poor obligations, and the like, and they used to laugh good-naturedly at my humorous misfortunes, but, after a time, Mrs. Bantock spoke sternly to me. "It's your own fault," she said. "You ought not to have run into debt. My husband tells me that, even in his poor days,"—she alluded to the £800 a year period, which lasted for two years—"he never owed a shilling." It occurred to me that, if I had had half Mr. Bantock's income in his poor days, I should not have owed a shilling, either, but I did not doubt she was right, and bowed my head meekly under the reproof.

But, with this exception, the Bantocks, I am sure, are full of keen, if silent, sympathy with the troubles of others. Not, however, that they encourage weak despair: they have the right, as bearing their own misfortunes so bravely, to expect the like of other people. "Crying does no good," I have heard Mrs. Bantock say. "Work is the only thing that will comfort you." To allege troubles as an excuse for failure in work seems contemptible to them. And, doubtless, they are right: indomitable pluck and the refusal to be beaten in life's battles are what make men and women strong and successful, and Mr. and Mrs. Bantock have often enforced this truth with wise and pithy precepts. They hold it almost criminal to encourage people in the opposite direction by pauperising charity. Mrs. Bantock has often given me much helpful encouragement when some disappointment has overtaken me. "Well, try again!" she says. "Work hard. Look at my husband, how bravely he goes on. You heard of that infamous mine? We all have to take a blow now and then." The mine in question had been expected largely to increase the Bantocks' income, but Mr. Bantock only just sold his shares in time to avoid loss; he made (he told me) only a few miserable thousands out of it. I was greatly comforted by his noble example of patience.

But perhaps I have enlarged enough on the Bantocks' virtues in misfortune. I hope I may have brought home the lesson which, in my humble way, I have tried to teach. And I do not wish to leave you with an impression of gloom and sorrow. If the Bantocks have their troubles, they have also much of the happiness and pleasure they so richly deserve; were it otherwise, one would indeed despair of the world. They have a share of good luck, also. Mr. Bantock's investments are often extremely lucky, and both he and Mrs. Bantock are often the recipients of legacies from relations. They grow richer every year, and every year strengthens their position among those whom England delights to honour. It is not — thank goodness! — mere titles and such irrational accidents that are valued nowadays, — we have ceased to be snobs, — it is people with solid merits and a solid stake in the country, like the Bantocks, who nowadays are valued; not merely rich people, again, but people with high principles and refined tastes. The Bantocks are more exclusive as time goes on; they think rightly that it is their duty not to waste their charming qualities on the first comer. Mr. Bantock

'er cared, modest man that he is,
rgo the fatigues of Parliament, but
is to go into it at an early date,
ll, no doubt, become a power in
ıd. There is talk of his being
1 to a duke's daughter.

amid the solemn circumstances
gh ambitions of their lives, the
ks are not without those domestic
ıose joys of kindly sympathy which
make beautiful the homes of ordi-
eople. The parents are happy in
votion of their children. Maud's
;e has, indeed, taken her away, in
, from her family, her husband,
, being perhaps not fully conscious
privilege of the connection. But
has never caused them a mo-
uneasiness; and if Tom and Ethel

Bantock gave her over a thousand pounds' worth of diamonds, and she, on his, gave him a new pair of carriage horses. Such simple kindness they value more than mere riches. Indeed, I must have written inadequately indeed if I have left you with any impression that the Bantocks care overmuch for money. They disproved that in the affair of Moss, and, indeed, they gaily depreciate their wealth and go so far as humorously to declare that they cannot afford this or that. Mrs. Bantock is always pleased when seats are given her for a theatre.

So I leave them in their troubles nobly borne and in their simple, beautiful pleasures. *Valeant*— until they haply ask me to dinner again. You join with me, I know, in my heartfelt wish for the continuance of their well-deserved prosperity.

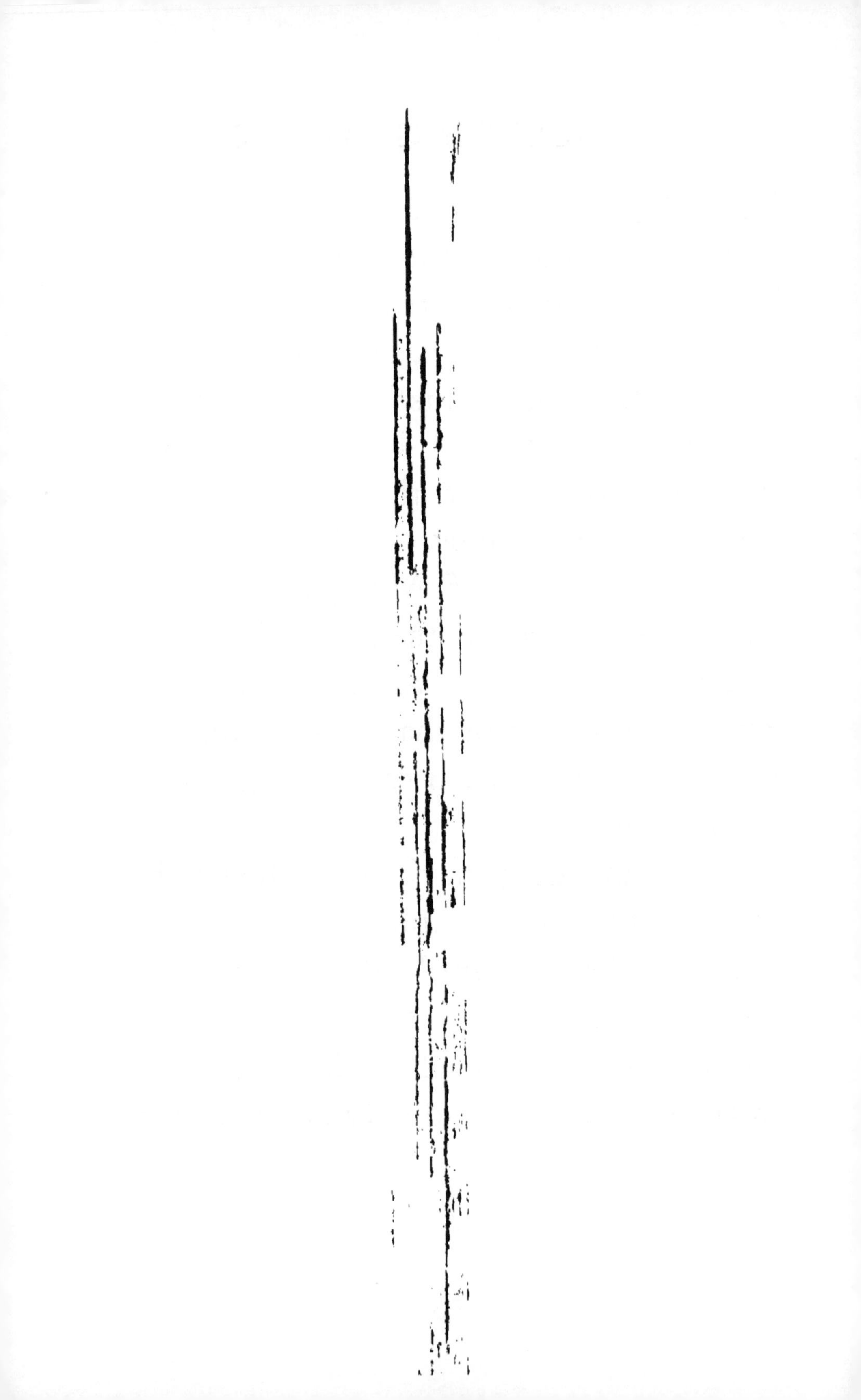

THE
BODLEY
HEAD
VIGO ST
W.

Telegrams
"BODLEIAN
LONDON"

TALOGUE *of* PUBLICATIONS
BELLES LETTRES

List of Books
IN
BELLES LETTRES
Published by John Lane
The Bodley Head
VIGO STREET, LONDON, W.

Adams (Francis).
ESSAYS IN MODERNITY. Crown 8vo. 5s. net.
A CHILD OF THE AGE. Crown 8vo. 3s. 6d. net.

A. E.
HOMEWARD: SONGS BY THE WAY. Sq. 16mo, wrappers. 1s. 6d. net. [*Second Edition.*
THE EARTH BREATH, AND OTHER POEMS. Sq. 16mo. 3s. 6d. net.

Æsop's Fables.
A HUNDRED FABLES OF. With 101 Full-page Illustrations by P. J. BILLINGHURST, and an Introductory Note by KENNETH GRAHAME. Fcap. 4to. 6s.

Aldrich (T. B.).
LATER LYRICS. Sm. fcap. 8vo. 2s. 6d. net.

Allen (Grant).
THE LOWER SLOPES: A Volume of Verse. Crown 8vo. 5s. net.
THE WOMAN WHO DID. Crown 8vo. 3s. 6d. net. [*Twenty-third Edition.*
THE BRITISH BARBARIANS. Crown 8vo 3s. 6d. net. [*Second Edition.*

Archer (William).
THE POETS OF THE YOUNGER GENERATION. With upwards of 20 Full-page Portraits after the original Wood Engravings of ROBERT BRYDEN. Demy 8vo. 16s. net. [*Shortly.*

Arnold (Matthew).
POEMS. With an Introduction by A. C. BENSON, and upwards of 70 Illustrations and a Cover Design by HENRY OSPOVAT. Crown 8vo. 6s. net.

Atherton (Gertrude).
PATIENCE SPARHAWK AND HER TIMES. Crown 8vo. 6s. [*Third Edition.*
THE CALIFORNIANS. Crown 8vo. 6s. [*Third Edition.*
SENATOR NORTH. A Novel. Crown 8vo.
THE DOOMSWOMAN. A Novel. Crown 8vo. 3s. 6d. [*New Edition.*

Bailey (J. C.).
ENGLISH ELEGIES. Crown 8vo. 5s. net.

Balfour (Marie Clothilde).
MARIS STELLA. Crown 8vo. 3s. 6d. net.
SONGS FROM A CORNER OF FRANCE. *See also* DES ECHEROLLES.

Barry (John D.).
THE ACROBAT. A Novel. Crown 8vo. 6s.

Beardsley (Aubrey).
EARLY WORK OF. Edited, with an Introduction, by H. C. MARILLIER. With over 180 Designs. Demy 4to. 31s. 6d. net. *Also a limited edition printed on Japanese vellum, at* 63s. net.

Beeching (Rev. H. C.).
IN A GARDEN: Poems. Crown 8vo. 5s. net.
ST. AUGUSTINE AT OSTIA Crown 8vo, wrappers. 1s. net.

Beerbohm (Max).
THE WORKS OF MAX BEERBOHM. With a Bibliography by JOHN LANE. Sq. 16mo. 4s. 6d net.
THE HAPPY HYPOCRITE. Sq. 16mo. 1s. net. [*Third Edition.*
MORE. Sq. 16mo. 4s. 6d. net [*Second Edition.*

Bell (J. J.).
THE NEW NOAH'S ARK. Illustrated in Colours. 4to. 3s. 6d.
JACK OF ALL TRADES. Illustrated by CHARLES ROBINSON. Fcap. 4to. 3s. 6d.

Bennett (E. A.).
A MAN FROM THE NORTH. Crown 8vo. 3s. 6d.
JOURNALISM FOR WOMEN: A Practical Guide. Sq. 16mo. 2s. 6d. net

Benson (Arthur Christopher).
LYRICS. Fcap. 8vo, buckram. 5s. net.
LORD VYET AND OTHER POEMS. Fcap. 8vo. 3s. 6d. net.
THE PROFESSOR AND OTHER POEMS. Crown 8vo, 5s. net.

Blunt (W. S.).
SATAN ABSOLVED; a Victorian Mystery. With a Frontispiece after G. F. WATTS, R.A. Pott 4to. 3s. 6d. net.

Bourne (George).
A YEAR'S EXILE. Crown 8vo. 3s. 6d.

Boyle (The Hon. Mrs.).
See E. V. B.

Bridges (Robert).
SUPPRESSED CHAPTERS AND OTHER BOOKISHNESS. Crown 8vo. 3s. 6d. net. [*Second Edition.*

Brotherton (Mary).
ROSEMARY FOR REMEMBRANCE. Fcap. 8vo. 3s. 6d. net.

Brown (Vincent).
MY BROTHER. Sq. 16mo. 2s. net.
ORDEAL BY COMPASSION. Crown 8vo. 3s. 6d.
TWO IN CAPTIVITY. Crown 8vo. 3s. 6d.
THE ROMANCE OF A RITUALIST. Crown 8vo. 6s.

Browning (Robert).
See FLOWERS OF PARNASSUS, page 15.

Buchan (John).
SCHOLAR GIPSIES. With 7 full-page Etchings by D. Y. CAMERON. Crown 8vo. 5s. net. [*Second Edition.*
MUSA PISCATRIX. With 6 Etchings by E. PHILIP PIMLOTT. Crown 8vo. 5s. net.
JOHN BURNET OF BARNS. A Romance. Crown 8vo. 6s.
GREY WEATHER. Crown 8vo 6s.
A LOST LADY OF OLD YEARS Crown 8vo. 6s.

Cadell (Mrs.).
RUBA'YAT OF OMAR KHAYAM. With an Introduction by Dr. GARNETT. 5s. net.

Campbell (Gerald).
THE JONESES AND THE ASTERISKS. A Story in Monologue. 6 Illustrations by F. H. TOWNSEND. Fcap. 8vo. 3s. 6d. net. [*Second Edition.*

Case (Robert H.).
ENGLISH EPITHALAMIES. Crown 8vo. 5s. net.

Castle (Mrs. Egerton).
MY LITTLE LADY ANNE. Sq. 16mo. 2s. net.

Chapman (Elizabeth Rachel).
MARRIAGE QUESTIONS IN MODERN FICTION. Crown 8vo. 3s. 6d. net

Charles (Joseph F.).
THE DUKE OF LINDEN. Crown 8vo 3s. 6d.

Cobb (Thomas).
CARPET COURTSHIP. Crown 8vo 3s. 6d.
MR. PASSINGHAM. Crown 8vo 3s. 6d.
THE JUDGMENT OF HELEN. NOVEL. Crown 8vo. 6s.
SEVERANCE. A Novel. Crown 8vo 6s.

Coleridge (Ernest Hartley)
POEMS. 3s. 6d. net.

Corvo (Baron).
STORIES TOTO TOLD ME. Square 16mo. 1s. net.
MORTAL IMMORTALS. Crown 8vo 6s.

Crane (Walter).

TOY BOOKS. Re-issue of.

This LITTLE PIG'S PICTURE BOOK, containing:

- I. THIS LITTLE PIG.
- II. THE FAIRY SHIP.
- III. KING LUCKIEBOY'S PARTY.

MOTHER HUBBARD'S PICTURE-BOOK, containing:

- IV. MOTHER HUBBARD.
- V. THE THREE BEARS.
- VI. THE ABSURD A. B. C.

CINDERELLA'S PICTURE BOOK, containing:

- VII. CINDERELLA.
- VIII. PUSS IN BOOTS.
- IX. VALENTINE AND ORSON.

RED RIDING HOOD'S PICTURE BOOK, containing:

- X. RED RIDING HOOD.
- XI. THE FORTY THIEVES.
- XII. JACK AND THE BEANSTALK.

BLUE BEARD'S PICTURE BOOK, containing:

- XIII. BLUE BEARD.
- XIV. THE SLEEPING BEAUTY.
- XV. BABY'S OWN ALPHABET.

Each Picture-Book containing three Toy Books, complete with end-papers and covers, together with collective titles, end-papers, decorative cloth cover, and newly written Preface by WALTER CRANE, 4s. 6d. The Twelve Parts as above may be had separately at 1s. each.

Crackanthorpe (Hubert).

VIGNETTES. A Miniature Journal of Whim and Sentiment. Fcap. 8vo, boards. 2s. 6d. net.

Craig (R. Manifold).

THE SACRIFICE OF FOOLS. Crown 8vo. 6s.

Croskey (Julian).

MAX. Crown 8vo. 6s. [*Second Edition.*

Crosse (Victoria).

THE WOMAN WHO DIDN'T. Crown 8vo. 3s. 6d. net. [*Third Edition.*

Custance (Olive).

OPALS: Poems. Fcap. 8vo. 3s. 6d. net.

Dalmon (C. W.).

SONG FAVOURS. Sq. 16mo. 3s. 6d. net.

D'Arcy (Ella).

MONOCHROMES. Crown 8vo. 3s. 6d. net.

THE BISHOP'S DILEMMA. Crown 8vo. 3s. 6d.

MODERN INSTANCES. Crown 8vo. 3s. 6d.

Davidson (John).

PLAYS: An Unhistorical Pastoral; A Romantic Farce; Bruce, a Chronicle Play; Smith, a Tragic Farce; Scaramouch in Naxos, a Pantomime. Small 4to. 7s. 6d. net.

FLEET STREET ECLOGUES. Fcap. 8vo, buckram. 4s. 6d. net. [*Third Edition*

FLEET STREET ECLOGUES. 2nd Series. Fcap. 8vo, buckram. 4s. 6d. net. [*Second Edition.*

A RANDOM ITINERARY. Fcap. 8vo. 5s. net.

BALLADS AND SONGS. Fcap. 8vo. 5s. net. [*Fourth Edition.*

NEW BALLADS. Fcap. 8vo. 4s. 6d. net. [*Second Edition.*

GODFRIDA. A Play. Fcap. 8vo. 5s. net.

THE LAST BALLAD AND OTHER POEMS. Fcap. 8vo. 4s. 6d. net.

Dawe (W. Carlton).

YELLOW AND WHITE. Crown 8vo. 3s. 6d. net.

KAKEMONOS. Crown 8vo. 3s. 6d. net.

Dawson (A. J.).

MERE SENTIMENT. Crown 8vo. 3s. 6d. net.

MIDDLE GREYNESS. Crown 8vo. 6s.

De Lyrienne (Richard).

THE QUEST OF THE GILT-EDGED GIRL. Sq. 16mo. 1s. net.

Des Echerolles (Mdlle.).

SIDELIGHTS ON THE REIGN OF TERROR. Translated from the French by M. C. BALFOUR. With Three Photogravures. Demy 8vo, gilt top. 12s. 6d. net.

De Tabley (Lord).

POEMS, DRAMATIC AND LYRICAL. By JOHN LEICESTER WARREN (Lord de Tabley). Five Illustrations and Cover by C. S. RICKETTS. Crown 8vo 7s. 6d. net. [*Third Edition*

POEMS, DRAMATIC AND LYRICAL. Second Series. Crown 8vo. 5s. net.

Devereux (Roy).

THE ASCENT OF WOMAN Crown 8vo. 3s. 6d. net.

Dick (Chas. Hill).

NINETEENTH CENTURY PASTORALS. Crown 8vo. 5s. net. [*In preparation*

Dix (Gertrude).

THE GIRL FROM THE FARM. Crown 8vo. 3s. 6d. net. [*Second Edition*.

Dostoievsky (F.).

POOR FOLK. Translated from the Russian by LENA MILMAN. With a Preface by GEORGE MOORE. Crown 8vo. 3s. 6d net.

Dowie (Menie Muriel).

SOME WHIMS OF FATE. Post 8vo. 2s. 6d. net.

Duer (Caroline, and Alice).

POEMS. Fcap. 8vo 3s. 6d. net.

Egerton (George).

KEYNOTES. Crown 8vo. 3s. 6d. net [*Eighth Edition*.

DISCORDS. Crown 8vo. 3s. 6d. net. [*Fifth Edition*.

SYMPHONIES. Crown 8vo. 6s. [*Second Edition*.

FANTASIAS. Crown 8vo. 3s. 6d.

THE HAZARD OF THE ILL. Crown 8vo. 6s. [*In preparation*.

Eglinton (John).

TWO ESSAYS ON THE REMNANT. Post 8vo, wrappers. 1s. 6d. net. [*Second Edition*.

E. V. B. (The Hon. Mrs. Boyle).

SEVEN GARDENS AND A PALACE. With Illustrations. Crown 8vo. 5s. net.

Farr (Florence).

THE DANCING FAUN. Crown 8vo. 3s. 6d. net.

Fea (Allan).

THE FLIGHT OF THE KING: A full, true, and particular account of the escape of His Most Sacred Majesty King Charles II. after the Battle of Worcester, with Sixteen Portraits in Photogravure and over 100 other Illustrations. Demy 8vo. 21s. net.

Field (Eugene).

THE LOVE AFFAIRS OF A BIBLIOMANIAC. Post 8vo. 3s. 6d. net.

LULLABY LAND: Songs of Childhood. Edited, with Introduction, by KENNETH GRAHAME. With 200 Illustrations by CHAS. ROBINSON. Uncut or gilt edges Crown 8vo. 6s.

Firth (George).

THE ADVENTURES OF A MARTYR'S BIBLE. Crown 8vo. 6s.

Fleming (George).

FOR PLAIN WOMEN ONLY. Fcap. 8vo. 3s. 6d. net.

Fletcher (J. S.).

THE WONDERFUL WAPENTAKE. By "A SON OF THE SOIL." With 18 Full-page Illustrations by J. A. SYMINGTON. Crown 8vo. 5s. 6d. net.

LIFE IN ARCADIA. With 20 Illustrations by PATTEN WILSON. Crown 8vo. 5s. net.

GOD'S FAILURES. Crown 8vo. 3s. 6d. net.

BALLADS OF REVOLT. Sq. 32mo. 2s. 6d. net.

THE MAKING OF MATTHIAS. With 40 Illustrations and Decorations by LUCY KEMP-WELCH. Crown 8vo. 5s.

Florilegium Latinum.

Celebrated Passages mostly from English Poets rendered into Latin. Edited by Rev. F. ST. JOHN THACKERAY and Rev. E. D. STONE. Crown 8vo. 7s. 6d. net.

Flowerdew (Herbert).

A CELIBATE'S WIFE. Crown 8vo. 6s. [*Second Edition*.

THE REALIST. Crown 8vo. 6s.

Ford (James L.).

THE LITERARY SHOP, AND OTHER TALES. Fcap 8vo. 3s. 6d. net.

Frederic (Harold).

MARCH HARES. Crown 8vo. 3s. 6d. net. [*Third Edition.*

MRS. ALBERT GRUNDY: OBSERVATIONS IN PHILISTIA. Fcap. 8vo. 3s. 6d. net. [*Second Edition.*

Fuller (H. B.).

THE PUPPET BOOTH. Twelve Plays. Crown 8vo. 4s. 6d. net.

Gale (Norman).

ORCHARD SONGS. Fcap. 8vo. 5s. net.

Garnett (Richard).

POEMS. Crown 8vo. 5s. net.

DANTE, PETRARCH, CAMOENS, cxxiv Sonnets, rendered in English. Crown 8vo. 5s. net.

Garstin (Norman).

THE SUITORS OF APRILLE. A Fairy Story. With 20 Full-page Illustrations and a Cover Design by CHARLES ROBINSON. Crown 8vo. 3s. 6d.

Geary (Sir Nevill).

A LAWYER'S WIFE. Crown 8vo. 6s. [*Second Edition.*

Gibson (Charles Dana).

DRAWINGS: Eighty-Five Large Cartoons. Oblong folio. 20s.

PICTURES OF PEOPLE. Eighty-Five Large Cartoons. Oblong folio. 20s.

LONDON: AS SEEN BY C. D. GIBSON. Text and Illustrations. Large folio, 12 × 18 inches. 20s.

THE PEOPLE OF DICKENS. Six Large Photogravures. Proof Impressions from Plates, in a Portfolio. 20s.

SKETCHES AND CARTOONS. Oblong Folio. 20s.

THE EDUCATION OF MR. PIPP. 80 Full-page Cartoons. Oblong folio. 20s.

Gilbert (Henry).

OF NECESSITY. Crown 8vo. 3s. 6d.

Gilliat-Smith (E.)

SONGS FROM PRUDENTIUS. Pott 4to. 5s. net.

Gleig (Charles)

WHEN ALL MEN STARVE. Crown 8vo. 3s. 6d.

THE EDGE OF HONESTY. Crown 8vo. 6s.

Gosse (Edmund).

THE LETTERS OF THOMAS LOVELL BEDDOES. Now first edited. Pott 8vo. 5s. net.

Grahame (Kenneth).

PAGAN PAPERS. Crown 8vo. 3s. 6d. net. [*Second Edition.*

THE GOLDEN AGE. Crown 8vo. 3s. 6d. net. [*Eighth Edition.*

DREAM DAYS. Crown 8vo. 3s. 6d. [*Second Edition.*

THE HEADSWOMAN. Sq. 16mo. 1s. net. (Bodley Booklets.)

THE GOLDEN AGE. With 19 Full-page Illustrations, numerous Ornaments, and a Cover Design by MAXFIELD PARRISH. Pott 4to 6s. net.

See EUGENE FIELD'S LULLABY LAND.

Gray (Thomas).

See FLOWERS OF PARNASSUS, p. 15.

Greene (G. A.).

ITALIAN LYRISTS OF TO-DAY. Translations in the original metres from about thirty-five living Italian poets, with bibliographical and biographical notes. Crown 8vo. 5s. net. [*Second Edition.*

Greenwood (Frederick).

IMAGINATION IN DREAMS. Crown 8vo. 5s. net.

Grimshaw (Beatrice Ethel).

BROKEN AWAY. Cr. 8vo. 3s. 6d. net.

Gwynn (Stephen).

THE REPENTANCE OF A PRIVATE SECRETARY. Crown 8vo. 3s. 6d.

THE DECAY OF SENSIBILITY, AND OTHER ESSAYS AND SKETCHES. Crown 8vo. 5s. net.

Hake (T. Gordon).

A SELECTION FROM HIS POEMS. Edited by Mrs. MEYNELL. With a Portrait after D. G. ROSSETTI. Crown 8vo. 5s. net.

Hansson (Laura M.).

MODERN WOMEN. An English rendering of "DAS BUCH DER FRAUEN" by HERMIONE RAMSDEN. Subjects: Sonia Kovalevsky, George Egerton, Eleanora Duse, Amalie Skram, Marie Bashkirtseff, A. Ch. Edgren Leffler. Crown 8vo. 3s. 6d. net.

Hansson (Laura M.)—*continued.*

We Women and our Authors. Translated from the German by Hermione Ramsden. Crown 8vo. 3s. 6d. net.

Hansson (Ola).

Young Opeg's Ditties. A Translation from the Swedish. By George Egerton. Crown 8vo. 3s. 6d. net.

Harland (Henry).

Grey Roses. Crown 8vo. 3s. 6d. net.

Comedies and Errors. Crown 8vo. 6s. [*Second Edition.*

The Cardinal's Snuff Box. A Novel. Crown 8vo. 6s.

Hawker (Robert Stephen, of Morwenstow).

The Complete Poetical Works. Crown 8vo. With Portrait. 7s. 6d. net.

Hay (Colonel John).

Poems including "The Pike County Ballads" (Author's Edition), with Portrait of the Author. Crown 8vo. 4s. 6d. net.

Castilian Days. Crown 8vo. 4s. 6d. net.

Speech at the Unveiling of the Bust of Sir Walter Scott in Westminster Abbey. With a Drawing of the Bust. Sq. 16mo. 1s. net.

Hayes (Alfred).

The Vale of Arden and Other Poems. Fcap. 8vo. 3s. 6d. net.

Hazlitt (William).

Liber Amoris; or, The New Pygmalion. Edited, with an Introduction, by Richard Le Gallienne. To which is added an exact transcript of the original MS., Mrs. Hazlitt's Diary in Scotland, and letters never before published. Portrait after Bewick, and facsimile letters. 400 Copies only. 4to, 364 pp., buckram. 21s. net.

Heinemann (William).

The First Step; A Dramatic Moment. Small 4to. 3s. 6d. net.

Summer Moths: A Play. Sm. 4to. 3s. 6d. net.

Helps (Sir Arthur).

The Spanish Conquest in America. New Edition. Edited by M. Oppenheim. 4 Vols. Crown 8vo. 3s. 6d. net.

Henniker (Florence).

In Scarlet and Grey. (With The Spectre of the Real by Florence Henniker and Thomas Hardy.) Crown 8vo. 3s. 6d. net. [*Second Edition.*

Herford (Oliver).

The Child's Primer of Natural History. With 48 Illustrations. 4to. 4s. 6d.

Hewlett (Maurice).

Pan and the Young Shepherd: A Pastoral. Crown 8vo. 3s. 6d. [*Second Edition.*

Hickson (Mrs. Murray).

Shadows of Life. Crown 8vo. 3s. 6d.

Hobbes (John Oliver).

Osbern and Ursyne. A Drama in Four Acts. Crown 8vo. 3s. 6d. net.

Holmes (Edmond).

The Silence of Love. Poems. Pott 4to. 3s. 6d. net. [*Second Edition.*

What is Poetry? An Essay. Pott 4to. 3s. 6d. net.

Hopper (Nora).

Ballads in Prose. Sm. 4to. 6s.

Under Quicken Boughs. Crown 8vo. 5s. net.

Housman (Clemence).

The Were Wolf. With 6 Illustrations by Laurence Housman. Sq. 16mo. 3s. 6d. net.

Housman (Laurence).

Green Arras: Poems. With 6 Illustrations, Title-page, Cover Design, and End Papers by the Author. Crown 8vo. 5s. net.

Gods and their Makers. Crown 8vo. 3s. 6d. net.

Irving (Laurence).

GODEFROI AND YOLANDE: A Play. Sm. 4to. 3s. 6d. net.

Jalland (G. H.).

THE SPORTING ADVENTURES OF MR. POPPLE. Coloured Plates. Oblong 4to, 14 × 10 inches. 6s.

James (W. P.).

ROMANTIC PROFESSIONS: A Volume of Essays. Crown 8vo. 5s. net.

Johnson (Lionel).

THE ART OF THOMAS HARDY: Six Essays. With Etched Portrait by WM. STRANG, and Bibliography by JOHN LANE. Crown 8vo. 5s. 6d. net. [*Second Edition.*

Johnson (Pauline).

WHITE WAMPUM: Poems. Crown 8vo. 5s. net.

Johnstone (C. E.).

BALLADS OF BOY AND BEAK. Sq. 32mo. 2s. net.

Kemble (E. W.).

KEMBLE'S COONS. 30 Drawings of Coloured Children and Southern Scenes. Oblong 4to. 6s.

A COON ALPHABET. 4to. 4s. 6d.

King (K. Douglas).

THE CHILD WHO WILL NEVER GROW OLD. Crown 8vo. 5s.

URSULA. A Novel. Crown 8vo. 6s.

King (Maud Egerton).

ROUND ABOUT A BRIGHTON COACH OFFICE. With over 30 Illustrations by LUCY KEMP-WELCH. Crown 8vo. 5s. net.

La Fontaine.

A HUNDRED FABLES OF. With 102 Illustrations and Cover Design by P. J. BILLINGHURST. Fcap. 4to. Linen. 6s.

Lander (Harry).

WEIGHED IN THE BALANCE. Crown 8vo. 6s.

Lane (C. H.).

ALL ABOUT DOGS: A Book for Doggie People. With 85 Full-page Illustrations, including nearly 70 Champions drawn from Life by R. H. MOORE. Demy 8vo. With a Cover Design by CARTON

Lark, The.

BOOK THE FIRST. Containing Nos. 1 to 12.

BOOK THE SECOND. Containing Nos. 13 to 24. With numerous Illustrations by GELETT BURGESS and Others. Small 4to. 25s. net. the set. [*All published.*

Leather (R. K.).

VERSES. 250 copies. Fcap. 8vo. 3s. net.

Lefroy (Edward Cracroft).

POEMS. With a Memoir by W. A. GILL, and a reprint of Mr. J. A. SYMONDS' Critical Essay on "Echoes from Theocritus." Cr. 8vo. Photogravure Portrait. 5s. net.

Lefroy (Ella Napier).

THE MAN'S CAUSE. Crown 8vo. 6s.

Le Gallienne (Richard).

PROSE FANCIES. With Portrait of the Author by WILSON STEER. Crown 8vo. 5s. net. [*Fourth Edition.*

THE BOOK BILLS OF NARCISSUS An Account rendered by RICHARD LE GALLIENNE. With a Frontispiece. Crown 8vo. 3s. 6d. net. [*Third Edition.*

ROBERT LOUIS STEVENSON, AN ELEGY, AND OTHER POEMS, MAINLY PERSONAL. Crown 8vo. 4s. 6d. net.

ENGLISH POEMS. Crown 8vo. 4s. 6d. net. [*Fourth Edition, revised.*

GEORGE MEREDITH: Some Characteristics. With a Bibliography (much enlarged) by JOHN LANE, portrait, &c. Crown 8vo. 5s. 6d. net. [*Fifth Edition, revised.*

THE RELIGION OF A LITERARY MAN. Crown 8vo. 3s. 6d. net. [*Fifth Thousand.*

RETROSPECTIVE REVIEWS, A LITERARY LOG, 1891-1895. 2 vols. Crown 8vo. 9s. net.

PROSE FANCIES (Second Series). Crown 8vo. 5s. net.

THE QUEST OF THE GOLDEN GIRL. Crown 8vo. 6s. [*Fifth Edition.*

THE ROMANCE OF ZION CHAPEL. Crown 8vo. 6s. [*Second Edition.*

Pennell (Elizabeth Robins).
THE FEASTS OF AUTOLYCUS: THE DIARY OF A GREEDY WOMAN. Fcap. 8vo. 3s. 6d. net.

Peters (Wm. Theodore).
POSIES OUT OF RINGS. Sq. 16mo. 2s. 6d. net.

Phillips (Stephen).
POEMS. With which is incorporated "CHRIST IN HADES." Crown 8vo. 4s. 6d. net. [*Fifth Edition.*
PAOLO AND FRANCESCA. A Play. Crown 8vo. 4s. 6d. net. [*Seventh Thousand.*
See also FLOWERS OF PARNASSUS, p. 16.

Pinkerton (T. A.).
SUN BEETLES. Crown 8vo. 3s. 6d.

Plarr (Victor).
IN THE DORIAN MOOD: Poems. Crown 8vo. 5s. net.

Pollard (E.).
BIRDS OF MY PARISH. Illustrated. Crown 8vo. 5s. net.

Posters in Miniature: over 250 reproductions of French, English and American Posters, with Introduction by EDWARD PENFIELD. Large crown 8vo. 5s. net.

Price (A. T. G.).
SIMPLICITY. Sq. 16mo. 2s. net.

Radford (Dollie).
SONGS AND OTHER VERSES. Fcap. 8vo. 4s. 6d. net.

Rands (W. B.).
LILLIPUT LYRICS. Edited by R. BRIMLEY JOHNSON. With 140 Illustrations by CHARLES ROBINSON. Crown 8vo. 6s.

Rhys (Ernest).
A LONDON ROSE AND OTHER RHYMES. Crown 8vo. 5s. net.

Richardson (E.).
SUN, MOON, AND STARS: PICTURES AND VERSES FOR CHILDREN. Demy 12mo. 2s. 6d.

Risley (R. V.).
THE SENTIMENTAL VIKINGS. Post 8vo. 2s. 6d. net.

Roberts (C. G. D.).
A SISTER TO EVANGELINE. A Romance. Crown 8vo. 6s.

Roberts (Harry).
THE CHRONICLE OF A CORNISH GARDEN. Illustrated. Crown 8vo. 5s. net.

Robertson (John M.).
NEW ESSAYS TOWARDS A CRITICAL METHOD. Crown 8vo. 6s. net.

Rosebery (Lord).
APPRECIATIONS AND ADDRESSES. Edited by CHARLES GEAKE. With Portrait. Cr. 8vo. 5s. net.

Russell (T. Baron).
A GUARDIAN OF THE POOR. Crown 8vo. 3s. 6d
THE MANDATE. Crown 8vo. 6s.

St. Cyres (Lord).
THE LITTLE FLOWERS OF ST. FRANCIS: A new rendering into English of the Fioretti di San Francesco. Crown 8vo. 5s. net. [*In preparation.*

St. John (Christopher).
THE CRIMSON WEED. A Novel. Crown 8vo. 6s.

Seaman (Owen).
THE BATTLE OF THE BAYS. Fcap. 8vo. 3s. 6d. net. [*Fourth Edition.*
HORACE AT CAMBRIDGE. Crown 8vo. 3s. 6d. net.
IN CAP AND BELLS. A Book of Verses. Fcap. 8vo. 3s. 6d. net. [*Fourth Edition.*

Sedgwick (Jane Minot).
SONGS FROM THE GREEK. Fcap. 8vo. 3s. 6d. net.

Setoun (Gabriel).
THE CHILD WORLD: Poems. With over 200 Illustrations by CHARLES ROBINSON. Crown 8vo, gilt edges or uncut. 6s.

Shakespeare's Sonnets.
With 14 Illustrations and Cover Design by H. OSPOVAT. Sq. 16mo 3s. 6d. net.

Sharp (Evelyn).

WYMPS: Fairy Tales. With 8 Coloured Illustrations by Mrs. PERCY DEARMER. Small 4to, decorated cover. 6s. [*Second Edition.* Also a New Edition, paper boards. 3s. 6d.

AT THE RELTON ARMS. Crown 8vo. 3s. 6d. net.

THE MAKING OF A PRIG. Crown 8vo. 6s.

ALL THE WAY TO FAIRY LAND. With 8 Coloured Illustrations by Mrs. PERCY DEARMER. Small 4to, decorated cover. 6s. [*Second Edition.*

THE OTHER SIDE OF THE SUN. Fairy Stories. With 8 Illustrations and a Cover Design in Colour by NELLIE SYRETT. Sm. 4to. 6s.

Shelley (Percy Bysshe and Elizabeth).

ORIGINAL POETRY. By VICTOR and CAZIRE. A reprint *verbatim et literatim* from the unique copy of the First Edition. Edited by Dr. GARNETT. Demy 8vo. 5s. net.

Shiel (M. P.).

PRINCE ZALESKI. Crown 8vo. 3s. 6d. net.

SHAPES IN THE FIRE. Crown 8vo. 3s. 6d. net.

Shore (Louisa).

POEMS. With an appreciation by FREDERIC HARRISON and a Portrait. Fcap. 8vo. 5s. net.

Shorter (Mrs. Clement) (Dora Sigerson).

THE FAIRY CHANGELING, AND OTHER POEMS. Crown 8vo. 3s. 6d. net.

Skram (Amalie).

PROFESSOR HIERONIMUS. Translated from the Danish by ALICE STRONACH and G. B. JACOBI. Crown 8vo. 6s.

Smith (John).

PLATONIC AFFECTIONS. Crown 8vo. 3s. 6d. net.

Stacpoole (H. de Vere).

PIERROT. Sq. 16mo. 2s. net.

DEATH, THE KNIGHT, AND THE LADY. Crown 8vo. 3s. 6d.

PIERETTE, HER BOOK. With 20 Illustrations by CHARLES ROBINSON. Crown 8vo. 6s.

Stevenson (Robert Louis).

PRINCE OTTO. A Rendering in French by EGERTON CASTLE Crown 8vo. 7s. 6d. net.

A CHILD'S GARDEN OF VERSES. With over 150 Illustrations by CHARLES ROBINSON. Crown 8vo. 5s. net. [*Fifth Edition.*

Stimson (F. J.).

KING NOANETT. A Romance of Devonshire Settlers in New England. With 12 Illustrations by HENRY SANDHAM. Crown 8vo. 6s

Stoddart (Thos. Tod).

THE DEATH WAKE. With an Introduction by ANDREW LANG. Fcap. 8vo. 5s. net.

Street (G. S.).

EPISODES. Post 8vo. 3s. net.

MINIATURES AND MOODS. Fcap. 8vo. 3s. net.

QUALES EGO: A FEW REMARKS, IN PARTICULAR AND AT LARGE. Fcap. 8vo. 3s. 6d. net.

THE AUTOBIOGRAPHY OF A BOY. Fcap. 8vo. 3s. 6d. net. [*Sixth Edition.*

THE WISE AND THE WAYWARD. Crown 8vo. 6s.

SOME NOTES OF A STRUGGLING GENIUS. Sq. 16mo, wrapper. 1s. net.

THE TRIALS OF THE BANTOCKS. Crown 8vo. 3s. 6d.

Sudermann (H.).

REGINA: OR, THE SINS OF THE FATHERS. A Translation of DER KATZENSTEG. By BEATRICE MARSHALL. Crown 8vo. 6s. [*Third Edition.*

Swettenham (Sir F. A.)

MALAY SKETCHES. Crown 8vo. 6s. [*Second Edition.*

UNADDRESSED LETTERS. Crown 8vo. 6s.

THE REAL MALAY: PEN PICTURES. Crown 8vo. 6s.

Lightning Source UK Ltd.
Milton Keynes UK
UKHW020809271218
334504UK00008B/434/P

9 780259 183181